Josh couldn't remember the last time he'd really smiled.

His sense of humor had been AWOL for months—years, maybe.

"Thank you," Clare said with a smile.

Without thinking, only needing to feel her warmth, he leaned in closer. "I don't know what to say," he murmured. He was hovering within an inch of those tantalizing lips, caught between a wish and a prayer.

"Say, 'You're welcome.'"

The soft whisper of air from her words fanned over his face as he closed his eyes and breathed her in. What would she do if he narrowed the gap between them and bent for a taste of those luscious lips?

He reached out and ended up grabbing a handful of air.

Hot damn. He should've known better.

Dear Reader,

June brings you four high-octane reads from Silhouette Romantic Suspense, just in time for summer. Steaming up your sunglasses is Nina Bruhns's hot romance, *Killer Temptation* (#1516), which is the first of a thrilling new trilogy, SEDUCTION SUMMER. In this series, a serial killer is murdering amorous couples on the beach and no lover is safe. You won't want to miss this sexy roller coaster ride! Stay tuned in July and August for Sheri WhiteFeather's and Cindy Dees's heart-thumping contributions, *Killer Passion* and *Killer Affair*.

USA TODAY bestselling author Marie Ferrarella enthralls readers with *Protecting His Witness* (#1515), the latest in her family saga, CAVANAUGH JUSTICE. Here, an undercover cop crosses paths with a secretive beauty who winds up being a witness to a mob killing. And then, can a single mother escape her vengeful ex *and* fall in love with her protector? Find out in Linda Conrad's *Safe with a Stranger* (#1517), the first book in her miniseries, THE SAFEKEEPERS, which weaves family, witchcraft and danger into an exciting read. Finally, crank up your air-conditioning as brand-new author Jill Sorenson raises temperatures with *Dangerous to Touch* (#1518), featuring a psychic heroine and lawman, who work on a murder case and uncover a wild attraction.

This month is all about finding love against the odds and those adventures lurking around every corner. So as you lounge on the beach or in your favorite chair, lose yourself in one of these gems from Silhouette Romantic Suspense!

Sincerely,

Patience Smith
Senior Editor

LINDA
CONRAD

Safe with a Stranger

Silhouette®
Romantic
SUSPENSE

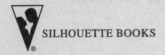

SILHOUETTE BOOKS
®

ISBN-13: 978-0-373-27587-8
ISBN-10:   0-373-27587-0

SAFE WITH A STRANGER

Visit Silhouette Books at www.eHarlequin.com

Printed in U.S.A.

LINDA CONRAD

was inspired by her mother, who gave her a deep love of storytelling. "Mom told me I was the best liar she ever knew. And that's saying something for a woman with an Irish storyteller's background," Linda says. Linda has been writing contemporary romances for Silhouette Books for seven years. Besides telling stories, her passions are her husband and family, and finding the time to read cozy mysteries and emotional love stories. Linda keeps busy and is happy living in the sunshine near the Florida Keys. Visit Linda's Web site at www.lindaconrad.com.

To all women everywhere: these books are for you.

And to Janet Capps, whose ideas for Texas-sounding
names were superior. Thanks to her, we found
Larado Hinojosa and the interesting character
behind the name. Thanks Janet!

Chapter 1

Nothing seemed off, yet everything felt wrong.

There were no eerie noises. No flashes of color. No lightning bolts to give her a clue. Still, Clare Chandler's instincts told her this funky Houston bus station was about to be the end of their road.

But she refused to give up. Frustration warred with determination as she clutched her sleeping son in her arms and slinked backward into the shadows. So, they would miss this bus. There would be another in a couple of hours.

The danger she'd felt had been coming from those two men there by the bus benches, the ones in the suits and ties. They looked legit, but slightly out of place. Had they come for her and Jimmy?

She'd been so careful. Hadn't used a credit card or a phone. Hadn't slipped up and called Jimmy by that hard-to-spell name his father had given him.

Clare and her son had only just arrived in this country on the private plane her old boss had helped to charter. There could not have been time for anyone to locate them.

Clare was sure she hadn't made any mistakes.

Nevertheless, her gut was telling her the worst had happened. She'd known her ex-husband, Ramzi, would come after them. After Jimmy. But she had hoped to reach the safety of her old college roommate's Missouri home first.

Trying to stand perfectly still so they wouldn't be spotted, Clare almost missed her two-year-old's muffled cry. She settled him higher against her shoulder. In her head she began clicking off the possibilities for his distress, wanting to be the best mother ever.

"Are you wet, Jimmy?" she asked and checked his diaper.

Her baby squirmed in her arms, wide-awake now. "No!" He didn't have many words in his vocabulary yet, but he knew what changing his diaper meant. She had very nearly managed to potty train Jimmy before it had been time to take her son and sneak away from the country of Abu Fujarah.

Ramzi had once said he thought she made a good mother, though that hadn't seemed good enough to make him want to let her raise her own son. Clare let out a beleaguered breath, then stiffened her spine, determined to do everything right.

Jimmy crammed his fist into his mouth and whined. Ah, he *was* hungry again. And he was tired. If she didn't do something about the hunger soon, he would start making a fuss. The last thing she needed was for Jimmy to throw a terrible-twos tantrum and draw the attention of everyone in the bus station.

Clare would never give up her son. Never. So she couldn't simply walk into the busy restaurant in the station and let those goons take him away. There had to be someplace else nearby where they could eat.

Murmuring to soothe Jimmy, she inched along the wall in an attempt to stay away from the harsh fluorescent lights of the station's main waiting room. She slipped out the side door into the starlight-spangled night.

Taking a breath of good ol' Texas air—the pungent, hit-you-in-the-face-with-gas-wells-and-feed-lots kind of air—Clare thought of her home. Maybe she should try calling her father in West Texas for help. She'd already rejected that plan once, knowing it would be the first place Ramzi would look for Jimmy. But right now, being home sounded so safe.

No, she didn't dare show up on her father's doorstep. Sticking with her plan to go to her old roommate's home would be for the best. She'd never mentioned Brenna to Ramzi and had hoped going in that direction would be the smartest idea for losing him and his men.

Clare checked the local neighborhood right outside the bus station's door and was dismayed at the sight of such a blighted area. This wasn't the kind of place for a woman and her child to go wandering after dark. But even going out there seemed a lot smarter than simply hanging around here waiting to be jumped.

Still holding tightly to Jimmy, Clare walked to the corner and checked in both directions. What looked like a roadhouse was down about a block from where she stood. Cars and trucks sat parked on every available inch of the parking lot, which seemed well lit and busy. If it was anything like the roadhouses and truck stops she remembered from West Texas, the place would at least serve food.

She knew joints like that usually served their share of hard liquor, too. But she would much rather take her chances with Texas drunks than with Ramzi's henchmen.

Josh Ryan wished he was well on his way to getting blitzed. He toyed with the idea of ordering a bottle of tequila, but managed to reject the thought. Just barely.

It wasn't only that he'd totally sworn off liquor sixty-three days, fourteen hours and twenty minutes ago. His grandfather had also recently died, and he was supposedly on his way to the funeral. It was a good five-hour drive there, and Josh had never been one for drinking and driving.

So what the hell was he even doing in this seedy bar, with its smell of burned ribs, cheap beer and fries cooking in lard? Twice so far he'd been approached by women in skimpy leather outfits who looked hungry and suggestive in a cheap way. Both times he'd sent them about their business with cold, dismissive looks.

If he'd been searching for oblivion tonight, he'd have found it by downing RedEye by the gallon and not with nameless, drugging sex.

But if it wasn't for booze or women, then why *was* he here? Apparently he was giving himself a test. Just to see if his new resolutions could stand up to the stress of the upcoming funeral. His life had become one big trial.

So far, the civilian world hadn't been what he'd hoped. Though he never would've re-upped—even if the army docs had said it would be all right. He wasn't *all right*. In Afghanistan, his concentration had deteriorated to a point where he had managed to get a buddy blown to hell and himself shot up bad. Once or twice in the heat of battle, he'd even come to the point of considering the use of one of his grandmother's so-called gifts. Amazing.

The white coats in the evac-hospital had eventually given h mental state some medical-sounding nonsense of a name an DX'd him out of the Rangers, sending him stateside. But Jos knew better. Post-traumatic stress disorder, hell. He'd ju stopped giving a crap whether he lived or died. His own li wasn't worth another bullet. And he refused to be put back in a place where what he did or didn't do meant someone else's lif

Never again.

He stared down at the remnants of his brisket sandwich ju as the jarring sound of a cue hitting a nest of pool balls cracke through the smoky air. A couple of cowpokes in the corner began to argue, while the laugh of an apparently very drunk woman tittered through the beer-soaked night.

It was time to go.

He paid the bill and shoved out the door into the parking lot. Even outside the night air was hard to take. Exhaust fumes and mesquite smoke mixed with the sulfur smell from nearby refineries over on the bayou. For the first time in many years, Josh was glad to be heading to deep south Texas.

There were a million things wrong with the south Texas town of Zavala Springs and the Delgado Ranch. But bad air had never been one of them.

The roadhouse parking lot was traffic central tonight. Pickup trucks of every size roared over the gravel. Giggly young girls squealed as their desperate-eyed oil-jockey dates grabbed their bottoms on the way to the bar's door. There weren't many like him who were leaving. But one or two Resistol-hatted twenty-somethings stumbled out the door on their way to the edge of the lot to puke their guts out.

God, he was so tired. This was no night for anything but a long, careful drive back to the Delgado.

Making his way to his old truck, Josh found he'd been blocked in by a brand-new Cadillac Escalade. He took a moment to wonder what the dude would do if he just backed into all that shiny black metal and made his own exit. Josh felt almost tired enough to give his family's *gifts* a shot in order to free his pickup.

Drawing in a breath instead, Josh went around the front of his truck and checked for another way out. It might be possible—*if* he went over an eight-inch-high curb stop. Then he'd be forced to drive over the next-door empty lot with all its broken glass and weeds growing upward through the old concrete. But damned if he didn't know his fifteen-year-old Ford F-150 could get through much worse.

He climbed into the pickup and started the engine. Rolling his front tires up and over the curb with minimum effort, he slowed as he realized he would have to gun it to get the back tires over, too.

Sitting at idle, Josh opened his side window and double-checked the position of his wheels. Yeah, it should work.

A high-pitched scream suddenly tore through the night air. The cry jolted him. Definitely coming from a female, it wasn't at all like the flirty shrieks those young girls made when their dates groped them in the dark.

No, this scream sounded like someone in trouble. Narrowing his lips in a frown, Josh figured it was none of his business. He had plenty of his own problems.

He shrugged a shoulder and jammed his foot down on the gas pedal, praying the old tread would hold together. A few seconds later he'd crossed the barrier and was slowing down on the other side in order to pick his way through the trash and glass scattered around the vacant lot.

Another scream, this time closer, captured his attention. He stepped on the brakes and searched the dark lot for any signs of trouble.

A figure appeared, illuminated in the distance by his head-lights. It was a female, all right. For a spilt second he saw a curvy form with a flash of blond hair. She seemed to be carrying something heavy. The vision dashed in and out of the beams.

Right on her tail were two greaseballs, dressed in suits with short haircuts. Their looks made Josh wonder if the FBI might be after this babe. But when he saw their drawn pistols, something in his brain snapped.

The picture was all wrong. No lawmen would run with guns out in the open like that, especially not when chasing an obviously unarmed woman.

Without another thought, Josh gunned his truck again and began chasing down the men. He used the Ford like he had his old mare back in the bronc-cutting days of his youth on the Delgado. But rounding up the two thugs turned out to be easier to manage than wild broncs had ever been.

Rooster-tailing it on the loose gravel as one of the men turned and tried to aim his pistol toward the truck, Josh sent a spray of caliche toward both guys, and they bolted. The two dudes headed away in the opposite direction as he nudged his bumper up close behind them. If they'd spilt up, one of them might've stood a chance at getting off a shot at him. But it turned out that neither of them was as bright as any year-old colt.

He wore the two creeps slick and left them panting and limping off the lot as they slithered back into the darkness behind the roadhouse. Then Josh spun his pickup and went after the girl.

With no clue as to what kind of trouble she was in, Josh should've just let it be. If he'd had a lick of sense, he would've been long gone down the road toward home by now. But nobody had ever referred to Josh Ryan as the most brilliant SOB in the world.

And besides…he'd become downright curious.

Clare slowed, trying to catch her breath. She couldn't believe her bad luck. She'd almost made it to the relative safety of the roadhouse when Ramzi's two goons spotted them.

They would've overtaken her and Jimmy, too, if it hadn't been for whoever it was in that old pickup. The fellow behind the wheel had driven like a maniac, but he'd done a fine job of blowing off the two thugs. It made her curious who her knight in scratched and dented armor might have been.

Now how was she going to get back to the bus station in time for the next bus? She couldn't get past the roadhouse without being seen by those men again.

With a cramp nagging at her side, she gulped for air and tried to think of a way out. Jimmy hadn't made a sound while she'd been running with him in her arms. But after she'd stopped, he began to squirm.

"Down, Mommy," he whined as he kicked at her stomach.

"Not here, honey," she said with a breathless gasp.

Her *no* didn't get through to the two-year-old. He kicked again, harder. At that same time the lifesaving pickup turned and came roaring up beside her.

She should have been frightened. Maybe she should have run in the other direction. Instead, her curiosity about what the fancy driver looked like had her standing on tiptoe and staring into the pickup's cab.

The guy leaned over and opened the passenger door. "Get in." All she caught of his face in the flash of the overhead light was a stubbled jaw and the brim of a beat-up Stetson pulled low over his eyes.

"What?" Belatedly she found her caution. "No."

"Look. Those dudes will be back here any second. And if you didn't notice, they have big, frigging guns. Get the hell in."

He was right. She was in no position to argue. Still… "I can't. But we should be okay thanks to you."

"Can't?"

This must have seemed like a good time to try to get his own way, because Jimmy squealed. When Clare tightened her grip around him, her child finally looked up at the pickup.

"Bye-bye," Jimmy said as he pointed toward the truck.

"Is that a kid?" The guy in the truck sounded incredulous.

"My son. I don't dare put him in your truck without the proper restraint. It isn't safe."

Just then, a loud ping resounded off the truck's back bumper. And a tiny spray of gravel exploded right next to the back rear tire.

"They're shooting now, lady. That ain't exactly *safe*. Climb in or not, but I'm getting the hell out of here."

Shooting? Ramzi would never allow anyone to shoot at his son. Just who were these goons, if not his men?

From that thought, it didn't take her a whole minute to load herself, her son and their duffel into the wide front seat of the pickup while the driver doused his headlights. "Go," she urged while still fumbling with the seat belt.

The driver took off with a crunch of tires against gravel. The whining engine strained to keep up with the man pouring on the gas. His takeoff bounced her around in the seat, but she hung on valiantly to Jimmy.

"Those city dudes are still on foot," the cowboy told her as he fought the wheel. "This old truck might not look like much, but it'll do zero to sixty in ten seconds. They won't stand a chance of getting to their vehicle or catching a glimpse of this truck in the dark before we're long gone."

Clare swallowed hard. She was grateful to this man, whoever he was. But she didn't want his crazy driving to end up taking any risks with Jimmy's life. After all, Ramzi's men couldn't possibly want to kill her son. They *must* just want to take him back to his father.

She thought of the bullets those goons had fired and amended that idea. They might not mind killing her to get to Jimmy.

"Can you go any faster?"

The man turned the lights back on and downshifted to take a corner. "Sugar, this heap may be fast off the line, but it won't hold together pushed to the limit."

He took four more corners in quick succession. When she'd gotten totally turned around and lost, he slowed down.

"They'll never make us now," he said. "So, you wanna tell me what the hell is going on? Why were those dudes after you?" He took one more corner, but this time on four wheels. "Tell me those *weren't* some sort of cops."

"Oh yeah," she said with a roll of her eyes. "Cops shoot at

women and children all the time—sure. I was just walking from the bus station to the roadhouse to get my son something to eat. How should I know those jokers?"

He shot her a quick glance before returning his attention to the road ahead. "It's after ten. Not exactly a terrific time to be waltzing around these streets with a baby. Isn't there a restaurant in the bus station?"

"Uh, I don't know," she lied.

"Yeah, I'll bet. And I suppose you have no idea why those guys were trying to get to you, either. All that drama seems extreme for a simple robbery."

"Well… Maybe they wanted to kidnap my little boy."

That shut him up for a few minutes. Finally, he cleared his throat and changed the subject. "You never made it to the roadhouse. I would've noticed you there. Is the kid still hungry?"

She looked down at Jimmy in her lap. "He and I both could use a little food. It's been a long time since we've eaten anything."

"You were planning on a bus trip, I'd guess. When's the bus leave?"

"Not until midnight."

"Then let's go find a decent place to eat. And I'll get you two back to the station in time."

Josh was kicking himself thirty ways from Sunday by the time he found a chain restaurant that stayed open all night. What the hell was he doing with a woman and a child? Only just now recovering from his idiot bout with alcohol, he didn't know about the long-term effects of PTSD. He still wasn't sure the docs were right where he was concerned.

He'd been planning on hanging with his baby sister in Zavala Springs for a while after the funeral. Just long enough for him to figure out what he wanted his life to be outside the Rangers and without the alcohol. He wasn't exactly great company.

Parking and shutting off the engine in the shadowed lot, Josh cleared his throat once more and tried to think of something civil to say.

The woman turned her face toward him and he caught the gleam of white teeth through the darkness. Hot damn, but her smile must have terrific wattage. He had a feeling she was going to turn out to be a real babe when he got a decent look at her in the lights.

"This'll be fine," she said. "Thanks for rescuing us. I think the least we can do is buy you dinner."

"Yeah? Well, I think I can manage on my own." Hell. Now he felt like a real jerk. What would've been wrong with letting her pay or saying something nice, like he'd already eaten?

Swinging down from the truck's cab, Josh hauled himself around the pickup to help lift her and the kid down. He wasn't sure why he automatically did that, but it seemed like the thing to do.

He ushered them into the relative safety of the well-lit restaurant and a hostess seated them. Without sitting, the woman excused herself to change the kid's diaper. It took another ten minutes to locate a high chair. This baby business seemed to be a real pain in the butt.

Finally all together in the booth, they'd placed their orders and now had coffee, iced tea and a sippy cup with juice sitting in front of them. It was then he took a moment and really looked across the table—and nearly bit his tongue in half.

Talk about a babe. He'd only gotten quick glances earlier because they'd been so busy, but this chick was a stunner.

Just looking at her was way better than eating the dessert he'd ordered and more fulfilling than any booze. Even better than the best barbecue he remembered his grandfather Will serving, the sight of Clare became food for the eyes. And sauce for the soul.

Her long, lush eyelashes covered clear, whiskey-colored eyes, and her silvery-blond streaked hair hung in a messy waterfall over the delicate curve of her shoulders. There was a tiny mole at the side of her luscious mouth, but it didn't mar the beauty of porcelain skin.

She rounded that mouth to say something to her son and the sight of those full, soft lips made him squirm. Whoo baby. For a man who hadn't cared one whit about sexy females in more years than he'd like to count, Josh was having full-blown wet dreams of her wrapping those lips around a body part of his that was right now sitting up and taking notice.

Hell.

"My son's name is Jimmy and I'm Clare Chandler," she said and held out her hand across the table.

He took it briefly. Just long enough to feel an electric shock of warmth running straight to his groin.

"Josh Ryan." Jerking back his hand, he noticed his words had been uttered in a much lower tone than normal.

"Do you live around here?"

He shook his head. "Don't live anywhere at the moment. Where're y'all from? Is that a West Texas drawl I hear?"

"Born and raised in Midland," she said and nodded. "But I haven't lived there for years."

It occurred to him then that she must have a husband around somewhere. Had she been his wife, he wouldn't have let her out of his sight. As for the kid... Well, as much as he didn't care for kids, and as much trouble as this one seemed, had Jimmy been his son he would've never trusted the two of them out alone.

"Where's home for you, then? Your husband waiting somewhere that you need to call?"

She glanced down at the table and then over at Jimmy. It took him a moment to notice, but her son definitely didn't have her coloring. Between her reaction to his question and the difference in their looks, Josh wondered if she was one of those new age single women who'd adopted a child without benefit of marriage or father.

"Jimmy's father and I are divorced. He's…in Europe. I'm bringing my baby back to the States to live."

Josh's gut was telling him something she'd said was a little off. Maybe a white lie. Whatever it was, he decided he needed to shed himself of these two in a hurry. He was becoming too intrigued by a pair of dewy amber eyes and a baby who reminded him too much of things that couldn't be.

They each ate what they'd ordered. She had a chef's salad, he had coffee with pecan pie and Jimmy had juice, a few bites of his mother's meat and cheese and enough saltine crackers to build a crumb-filled castle.

"Hope that'll hold y'all for a while," he said. "It's nearly time to get you two back to the bus station."

He'd rather not learn any more about her or hang around her kid any longer than necessary. It was already past time to be on the road again.

"Yes, I agree. Those two goons should've given up and left by now." She began packing up Jimmy's things. "Our bus leaves in a half hour."

They made their way back to the truck and he settled them in before he climbed behind the wheel again. On the way back he kept sneaking looks at her when she wasn't paying attention.

She was a stunner, all right. With neat khaki pants, a form-fitting brownish-colored top and a light suede jacket, her curves weren't obnoxious or too obvious. But they were definitely in all the right places. The gaze from her bright eyes darted down to Jimmy and then back out the windshield, always checking. And that danged silken strand of blond hair still dangled over one of her shoulders as if it was just begging to be played with.

Something nagged at him. Though her clothes weren't overtly expensive and her manner wasn't snooty, Clare just seemed to ooze sophistication. She had a worldly character about her.

So what was she doing taking a bus? And what had those two suits really wanted with her and the kid?

Stuff those thoughts. He didn't want to get any more involved than he'd already become. All he wanted was to get the both of them on their way and then wash his hands of the whole damn puzzle.

Josh drove around the bus station twice, trying to be sure the suits weren't still hanging around outside. He spotted Clare's bus parked at an outdoor gate, already loading and with a long line of passengers waiting to climb on. The two of them wouldn't even have to walk through the station to board.

"I'm not going to get out," he told her as he idled by the curb. "I'll just drop y'all off. You'll be okay, right?"

He couldn't wait until she got out of his truck. The sexy vibes she'd been throwing off were a distraction, and he needed that about as much as another hole in the head.

She nodded as she unbuckled and prepared herself and her son to go. "Sure. We really have to thank you again for all you did for us. I don't think we would've made it without you, and I wish there was something more I could do to say thanks."

The various ways he could think of were not suitable to say aloud to a near stranger. "No problem. Take care of yourself and Jimmy, ya hear?"

Josh watched as she carried the toddler to the end of the line. She looked vulnerable. Vulnerable, worldly and sexy. What a strange combination. He didn't think he'd ever met anyone like that before in his entire life.

While he sat in the pickup with his tongue hanging out and watched as her line inched toward the bus door, two dark figures came out of nowhere and grabbed her and Jimmy. The same two dudes who'd tried and failed at the roadhouse. Ah, hell!

He was out of the truck in an instant.

Chapter 2

Running full out, Josh reached them in time to lunge at one of the bad guys. That one took a swing and caught Josh hard on the chin, and then the same dude spun, hoisting Jimmy in his arms as he took off.

"Jimmy!" Clare shouted while fighting the other guy.

Before Josh could intervene, she stomped her foot on the goon's instep, shoved her open palm up under his chin and then rammed her knee into his groin. That guy crumbled, and Josh took off after the one with Jimmy.

Josh caught up to him with no trouble. But slowing the slimeball down without hurting the kid in his arms was tough. Josh finally had the guy in a choke hold at about the same time as Jimmy started squealing and squirming. The boy wiggled like a greased calf at a fair, which seemed to confuse the goon, who couldn't hang on to the kid.

Josh used the opportunity to take his shot, poking his fingers hard into the guy's eye sockets while jerking Jimmy from his grip with the other hand. Josh didn't spend time gloating over his handiwork, just tore back toward the bus and Clare with Jimmy thrown over his shoulder.

"Jimmy, thank heaven," she sobbed when Josh reached her. Relief and gratitude filled her eyes.

"Let's go." He grabbed her elbow, heading outside.

"Go where?"

"Anywhere but here. Get in the truck. Y'all are safer with me than on that danged bus, no matter where we end up."

After about a half hour of silently driving in circles, trying to lose the goons for sure, Josh thought better of his last remarks. "So where were y'all headed? Is there some other way you can get to wherever you're going?"

Clare turned to him, the tension in her face clear and alarming. "Um…"

Well, that wasn't much of an answer. In fact, this babe had been real slow coming up with any straight answers. He doubted that a word she'd said since the moment they'd met had been on the level. Well, he'd had enough.

Josh spotted an all-night discount department store in the next block. The huge lot was busy with people coming and going and he figured they could join up and get lost in the crowd of trucks. He pulled in under the low-hanging branches of a willow and shut down the engine.

"What are we doing here?" Clare softly asked.

When he turned to answer her, the sight he beheld left him flabbergasted and holding his breath. There, through the low light and in the passenger seat of his old beat-up pickup, sat the most beautiful woman he'd ever seen holding a sleeping angel in her lap. Was it just a trick of lighting that made her suddenly look like a Madonna? Her skin was exquisite, like fine china. Every strand of her hair lay in silky perfection. Her nose wasn't too small or too large, but just right. And her long lashes lay against high cheekbones as she gazed down at the babe in her arms.

Josh swallowed hard against the lump in his throat.

The mother and child made such a compelling picture that Josh wished he knew how to draw. He'd never been an artist, and he wasn't sure that even a Michelangelo could manage to capture the perfect essence of this mother and child.

His heart ached for all the pictures like this one that he would miss seeing in his lifetime. The pictures of a loving spouse and child that he would never have—and that his brother and sister would miss having in their lives, as well. Those thoughts sobered him, left him melancholy and finally made him angry. Exactly the way he'd spent the last fifteen years of his life. Mad as hell with no way to let it loose and no one to take it out on.

But Josh wasn't the kind to dwell on his troubles for very long. He was much more an action kind of guy. Kick butts, take names and take charge. It was the way he'd operated for most of his life. So, burying his personal problems like always, he decided to focus on Clare's troubles instead.

"We need to talk." He swiveled to a position in his seat where he could watch her face as he questioned her. "I want answers about what the hell is going on. And don't give me any of that bull about not knowing those two sleazy dudes or why they were after you. I've been shot at, sucker punched and chased tonight, and I want to know why."

Clare didn't know what to do or say to answer his questions. She didn't know who to rely on. Was Josh someone to trust? Did she dare?

She kept perfectly still and stared at the man who was for all purposes a complete stranger. But as the flickering light from one of the parking-lot lamps filtered through the windshield and seemed to water down the edges of his face with soft gray tones and shadows, her insides softened toward him, too.

The look in his eyes as he glared at her wasn't stony or cynical or in any way threatening, despite his rough words. No, Josh's facial expression seemed to reach out to her with unspoken compassion. And with something—warmer, more focused—underlying that. Clare didn't want to think too much about the underlying heat. By now her own body was suffering from a wave of warmth just staring at his remarkably deep-set eyes and intense chocolate-colored gaze.

He was easy to look at. And hot! Six-two or -three, she'd have to guess. All of that was lean, hard-packed muscle. Not the kind of muscle you saw in the gym, but the real sinew and form of an outdoorsman who didn't hesitate to use his body. He was wearing camo pants and a tight-fitting black T-shirt. Old cowboy boots and a Stetson completed the picture. And what a picture it was, too.

She drew in a shaky breath and her supposedly quick brain finally kicked into gear as she remembered that without his help, Jimmy would have been lost. And she would be hopeless. Even not knowing a thing about her, Josh had given her the sweetest gift in the world.

She swallowed carefully, deciding that she needed someone's help and it might as well be his. "It's a long story."

"I've got all night. I don't have to be anywhere until the day after tomorrow."

"Oh." The way he'd said that, with a murmur of sorrow in his voice, made her curious to know where he was headed. But she figured she owed him the first explanations.

She shifted Jimmy in her arms and rolled her window down halfway for some air. "Okay," she began, wondering how she could put all her embarrassment and terror into words. "But this has to be off the record."

"Wait a sec," he interrupted. "Stay put and hold that thought. I'll be right back."

"Wha…" Before she could get a word out, he'd ripped the keys from the ignition, unbuckled and stepped out of the truck into the humidity and heat of an East Texas night.

"Keep the doors locked and an eye out," he told her. "I'll be back in a few minutes. You two should be fine."

He slammed the door, locked it behind him and stalked off toward the discount store, leaving her with her mouth open and her head shaking. What was with this guy?

True to his word, and before she had a chance to rethink her tenuous position and climb out of his truck and disappear, Josh was already headed back in her direction. And he was carrying an enormous box with him.

"What in blazes…"

"It's a car seat for a two-year-old," he said after he opened the door. "Sorry I took so long but I had to get a complete briefing on its installation. Can you put the kid down there on the front seat without waking him up and get out a minute? I'll give you the short course as we tuck it into the backseat."

"What backseat?"

Josh slanted a grin in her direction. It was the first one she'd seen from him and it made her heart stutter with lust and longing. Wow. That was fast work. She didn't even know where she and Jimmy would be in the next hour, yet here she was, thinking about a near stranger in terms of a heated grin. Damn it. She was a mother, for heaven's sake.

Lightly slipping out of the front seat and easing Jimmy down, Clare tried to get herself back together. This was serious business. Jimmy's whole future was riding on her doing everything right.

"Lucille has a backseat," he told her as he pulled a folding knife from his pocket and set to work opening the box. "Maybe it's more of a bench than a real seat, but this child-size car seat will fit just fine."

"Lucille? Your truck has a name?" She'd never met anyone who'd named their vehicle. It seemed a little eccentric for such a take-charge guy.

"Yeah. I saved to buy her before I signed up for the army, and then afterward made a few modifications in my spare time. I had a buddy who took care of her for me while I was out of country. She may not be a lot to look at, but she still runs good enough to keep us both out of trouble."

He and his truck *had* saved her and Jimmy from a world of trouble. She decided it was worth the effort to become real close friends with Lucille. And to give the man who owned her a break.

Clare and Josh finished installing the child safety seat and then she gently laid Jimmy down into it and buckled him in without waking him up. Grateful not to have awoken the baby, the two adults climbed back into the front and gingerly closed their doors.

"Thanks," she whispered. "But you didn't have to spend so much on us. We'll be back out of your way just as soon as I can figure out what to do."

"The kid was beginning to look a little heavy in your arms. I thought maybe you both needed a break and some space. You could always use that same seat in an airplane or a rental car if need be." He handed her one of the water bottles he'd brought back with the car seat.

The bottle was cold and dripping sweat and she was thrilled to be able to quench her thirst. "Thanks. But I'll pay you back for the seat." She swallowed a slug of the water and immediately felt better. "This is wonderful."

Clare thought once again about all that Josh had done for them. She was still rather hesitant to trust a person whom she'd just met for the first time a few hours ago—especially a man who made her itchy and prickly by simply looking in her direction.

After all, she'd recently escaped from one gigantic mistake made solely on lust, and she didn't dare dive off that cliff blindly into another one.

But at the moment, there wasn't time for careful consideration. Ramzi's men, or whoever those goons had been, might catch up to them anytime. They weren't safe yet, and wouldn't be until they were well on their way out of town.

Her reporter's instincts were telling her that Josh could not possibly hurt her or her child. Clare understood the Texas men she'd been raised with. They called a spade a spade. They were loyal to a fault, and always more than generous and fair. Her father was a good example, and Josh, too, appeared to be among the best of the breed.

Josh shot her a wary look over the top of his own water bottle. "You ready now to give up those explanations?"

"I think maybe there's only time enough for the bullet points—the headlines. Okay?"

He nodded and sat back against the door to wait.

"You know, I'm really not sure who those men were who attacked us."

Josh narrowed his eyes and frowned.

"Well, I thought I knew, but…" She took another sip of water. "Okay. Okay. Here's the background.

"About three years ago I married a Middle-Eastern man whom I thought I loved. He was…" Clare looked over at Josh and realized her original lust-filled thoughts about Ramzi had been so far off the mark that it would sound ridiculous trying to explain. "Well, anyway, he wasn't what he appeared to be. For the first six months or so things seemed great between us. I continued to work—"

"What kind of work?" Josh interrupted.

"I'm a reporter. Magazine bylines mostly. I was working for the *Oil News Monthly* when I met him. And since he was also busy at the time working as an undersecretary for OPEC, I just kept on doing what I'd been doing—traveling and getting interviews for my job." She took a breath as gentle memories snuck into her mind and threw her out of rhythm for a minute. "We'd meet up on our weekends off and for whirlwind vacations in places like Corfu and the beach resort on Phuket, Thailand. It all seemed…terribly romantic."

"Uh-huh. So what happened?"

"Jimmy." Clare snapped back to reality in an instant. "I mean, I learned I was pregnant with Jimmy and everything changed. My husband insisted I quit working until the baby was born and he took me back to his home country…ostensibly to met his family and have their doctors check me over. He claimed their physicians were the best that money could buy. I knew he was concerned for our baby's health, so I agreed."

"So what really went down when you got there?" Josh finished his water bottle and stashed the empty under the seat.

This was where the truth was more than a little embarrassing. Clare wished she could fudge on the answer, but fudging wasn't the way she'd been raised. It wasn't who she was. So she straightened up in her seat and set her chin.

"For one thing, I found out that I hadn't done quite enough of a background check before I got married. Apparently I was so smitten, I forgot the first rule to getting a good story. Check your facts. It turns out that my husband already had a few current wives stashed away back in his homeland."

"A few? *Current?* How many?"

"Eight."

Josh's eyes widened. "So what did you do when you found out? Did you divorce him then?"

"I would've. Or I would've left and come back to Texas to have my child. But by that time Ramzi had fixed things with the local authorities to keep me in his country and married to him for as long as he wished. Women have no rights there. They're their husband's property. I finally woke up and realized what a mess I was in, but by then it was too late. Not even the U.S. State Department could help me."

"This sounds like a bad movie plot. How'd you get free?"

Her life did sound a lot like a grade-B movie now that she thought about it. She decided to speed up the rest of the story.

"Ramzi suddenly became willing to divorce me when the baby was a year and a half. In fact, he wanted to have me deported. To be sent home and out of his way. But he wasn't about to let Jimmy leave the country."

Josh looked a little confused. "He wanted you gone…without your baby?"

"Yep. He convinced a judge that his other wives could do a better job of raising Jimmy in the Abu Fujarah tradition."

"And a judge bought that? That a mother shouldn't be allowed to raise her own son?"

Clare remembered how incensed she'd been. "The judge was one of Ramzi's cousins and was probably on his father's payroll."

"Your ex has rich parents?"

"Very. They control most of the oil in their oil-rich nation. And they control most of the people there, too."

Josh's eyes narrowed and his lips drew together in a thin white line. He seemed to be taking this story personally, and Clare wished she understood why.

"I'm positive Ramzi will try to find Jimmy and take him back to his country," she told him in a rush. "I don't think Ramzi gives a flip about what happens to me, but Jimmy is his only son. I know he wants him and probably won't rest until he gets him back."

Would Josh think she was terrible for taking her son away from his father? Maybe. And maybe she felt a little bit guilty about that herself.

"I wouldn't mind letting them visit with each other," she added. "But I can't lose my son forever. I can't."

Jimmy stirred in the backseat. Clare got on her knees and leaned over to check on her son. Josh needed a moment to let her story sink in. But as he turned to glance back at the baby, he caught a view that stopped him cold. Clare's fashionable khaki slacks had pulled tight against the rounded curve of her bottom, and he was lost in a sudden flash of fantasy.

The outline of her bikini underwear was easy to trace under the slacks. Lordy mercy, but it had been forever since he'd seen a woman's underwear. Or since he'd taken that same underwear off and enjoyed the fruit of the woman beneath. He hadn't even given sex much thought lately, he'd been so wrapped up in other problems. To be more precise, since before he'd been in that fire-fight back in Afghanistan. The one that had taken his buddy's life and landed Josh in the hospital and out of the Rangers for good.

Forcing his eyes away from the temptation in front of him, he tried to focus on the problem at hand. What would he be doing if he were in Clare's place? Then again, what would he have done if he'd been in her ex-husband's place?

If he'd been in Clare's shoes, he would've done the same thing as she had. No question. But if he'd been in her ex-husband's place, well… Different culture or not, Josh would never try to tear a child away from its mother.

"So you think those goons at the bus station were sent by your ex to kidnap your son?" he asked as Jimmy quieted down and she turned back around in the seat.

She nodded and set her mouth in a determined line. "Yes. At least, I did until they started shooting. I can't believe that Ramzi would actually allow anyone to shoot at and possibly harm his son. Whatever else he is or does, my ex-husband loves Jimmy. I'm sure of it."

"But you have no other ideas as to who those two suits might've been? Other than working for your ex, I mean."

"None at all."

"Then I think we have to assume that's who they were. I guess it's possible they weren't really shooting at you back there. Maybe they were aiming at the truck's tires. I did notice they weren't the best shots in the world."

Clare actually smiled at that, and Josh's heart skipped a beat. Man, he'd never been so taken with anyone so fast in his life. Too fast or not, he knew in that instant he would do just about anything to keep her and her child safe.

"Okay. So, let's talk about what you want to do from here," he said with a little determination of his own clear in his voice. "You need a plan."

An hour later they sat in a parked Lucille outside one of the rental-car agencies on the outskirts of the airport. They were waiting for the agents to come to work for the day at 5:00 a.m. Clare seemed convinced that driving to her old roommate's home in Missouri was her best course of action. Josh wasn't so sure.

He didn't like the idea of her traveling so far with the baby alone. What if those goons caught up to them? She already looked about ready to drop. How was she going to drive herself and her child any distance at all, let alone to a city that was at least a twelve-hour drive away?

"Don't you think you should contact your friend before you and Jimmy just turn up on her doorstep?" he asked as she changed her son's diaper. "What if she's out of town for business or on vacation or something?"

Clare looked up at him from under those spiky, blond lashes. "Maybe I should. It never occurred to me that she might not be there. Have you got a phone?"

He shook his head. "Sorry. Traveling light."

"Me, too. Ramzi took all my electronics away while I was under his roof," she admitted bluntly. "I'll have to start all over again once I'm back home. But for now, I can call from a pay phone inside the rental agency."

In a few minutes the rental agents arrived and opened up for the day. "Here," she said as she turned to Josh with Jimmy in her arms. "You hold the baby while I go in and call Brenna. If everything's okay, I'll rent the car and be right back."

Josh found himself in the spot where he'd never imagined he would be. Holding a toddler in his arms. Jimmy was still a little groggy from sleep and the baby leaned his head against Josh's shoulder.

The yearning for a child of his own stole over Josh like the shadow of a cloud on a sunny day. He fidgeted slightly, not sure how to hold a kid, and not wanting to face the old pain of his family's loss. For years he'd successfully avoided thinking about the curse. Just as he had successfully avoided being around kids.

Now he was stuck with both. Damn it.

He took off his hat and propped himself against the pickup as Jimmy blinked open his eyes and looked up at the man who was holding him in his arms. "Da De?" the baby murmured sleepily as he patted the overnight stubble on Josh's cheek.

"No, boy," Josh whispered. "I'm not your daddy. I'm not anybody's daddy." Saying it aloud brought back the old stinging regret. Josh ignored the ache as he'd always done before and did what he had to do to get by.

"But I'll take care of you, son. Don't you fret." He would make sure this kid and his mother were safe—even if he had to use some of his grandmother's magic to make it so.

"Josh!" Clare came running out of the agency office. "Oh. My. God. They're there. In Missouri."

She was out of breath and her face was pale and drawn. "A couple of Ramzi's men have somehow already found Brenna.

They're waiting outside her house for Jimmy and me to show up. We can't go to her for help. She was my best hope. What'll we do?"

No problem there. "Climb back into Lucille. They can't have *her* plate numbers and won't be able to find us. You two will be safe with me. I won't let anything happen."

It was a promise he meant to keep. No matter what.

Chapter 3

"But where can we go? Where can we hide that they can't find us?" Clare knew her voice sounded high-pitched and panicked. She felt herself falling over the edge into hysteria.

Josh started the pickup, and the good ol' girl rumbled as he turned to speak. "This ex of yours apparently has a lot of pull— and a lot of money. Am I right?"

Clare nodded her head, but the words wouldn't come. All her plans were going up in a blaze. Every idea she'd had for saving herself and her son looked like a dead end.

"So I'm guessing he can probably get a line on anybody you've ever known in your past. That means you and Jimmy can't go to your old addresses or to any of your old friends or family." Josh said the words easily, like a statement of fact, but he sure looked as unhappy about their meaning as she felt.

Calm. She had to remain calm. For Jimmy's sake.

"I—I— Exactly right," she stuttered breathlessly.

"Then I can't figure any other way out. You and Jimmy have no choice but to stick with me.

"Your ex doesn't know who I am," Josh added after a moment. "You and I didn't know each other in the past. And…" He shook his head and set his mouth. "None of us seems to have any choice."

"But stick with you to go where?" Clare knew the time had come to make a decision about Josh, but she just wished she'd been allowed more of an opportunity to get to know him. "You said you didn't live anywhere at the moment. Where were you headed when you ran into us?"

Josh grimaced, put the truck into gear and pulled out of the parking lot. "I was raised in south Texas, near the town of Zavala Springs. I was headed back there…to my grandfather's funeral."

"Oh. I'm sorry to hear that." So that was what the sadness in his voice had been all about. She'd known it must be something bad. "But Jimmy and I don't want to intrude on your family's time of sorrow. And, anyway, just going off with you doesn't solve the real problem. Eventually I'll have to face Ramzi again. Jimmy is his son, and the two of us will never be safe until the U.S. government gives us their protection under the law."

Josh gave her a look that said, Too late. The decision has been made. Then he turned the truck at the next corner and headed up the on-ramp to Interstate 610 West.

"You got any better ideas, speak up." He was focused on the highway ahead, chin set. "My brother and sister will be at the funeral, and they've both got good contacts. My brother even works for the feds. Maybe one of the two of them will have an idea of how you can set yourself free of the mess you've managed to make."

Clare opened her mouth to utter a smart retort to his zinger, but fortunately remembered in time that she and Jimmy really were in a huge mess. She slammed her lips shut before saying something that would put her into even deeper trouble. At least she wasn't so panicked anymore. Folding her arms across her chest, Clare decided to sit back and fume instead.

He was right. There was no choice.

Josh wasn't quite sure why he'd been so rude. Clare had enough trouble in her life right now; she didn't need him snapping at her, too. But she'd been looking at him with an expression on her face that said she thought he was some kind of hero. He was no hero—far from it. So he'd decided to show her exactly how unheroic he could be.

Smart as hell, Ryan. Nice work. As usual.

It wasn't as if he didn't like her or didn't have a high opinion of what she'd done so far. He did. Finding a way to get her and Jimmy out of a tradition-bound and male-dominated foreign country, and then managing to protect her child through all kinds of dangers, was admirable. Obviously she had a mother tiger's instincts. This was no fainting flower of a woman. Tough and determined, she was a fighter, and how he would dearly love to have her go a few rounds with him.

All of a sudden his thoughts began stirring emotions inside him that made him cower. Things that felt so strong, he'd never experienced anything like them before. Prickling and gut-wrenching, they nearly brought tears to his eyes. The simple truth was, he wanted his own family. Badly, damn it. Life was unfair. At least, *his* life.

But before he could stem the unwanted emotions and shove them back down where they wouldn't get in his way, he found himself angry all over again. And since it had been his admiration of Clare that had started stirring the whirlwind of emotion in his gut, she was bound to be the object of his anger.

Crap. He hadn't wanted things to go down this way. Josh had never imagined, when he saved them, that he would get stuck with the two runaways. At first he'd had no intention of taking

Clare and Jimmy with him anywhere, and the idea of bringing them along to Zavala Springs had been the furthest thing from his mind. After all, he barely wanted to go back there to face the past himself. He sure as hell didn't want to drag her and the baby along to mingle with his old ghosts, too. No way would he take a chance of her finding out about his family's bizarre history.

But what was he supposed to do with them? He couldn't just dump a woman and a baby by the side of the road. Certainly not this woman and child. So he bit back his temper once again and stepped down on the gas pedal.

Clare made a little snuffling noise and he shot a furious glance in her direction. Her arms were hugging her chest and those fancy, full lips of hers were all stuck out in a huff. Shoot. Another more urgent and surprising sizzle of awareness clipped him in the gut without warning.

Suddenly the urge to kiss her senseless swamped him with such a need that he wasn't sure he could tame it. Danged woman! This kind of aggravation was more than he could stand at the moment. How had his life taken such a drastic turn in only a few short hours?

Gritting his teeth and forcing his gaze back out the windshield where it belonged, Josh noticed that the lavender and gray tones of the coming dawn had begun to lighten the morning sky and give shape to their surroundings. A new day had begun over southeast Texas. Breathe, he admonished himself. Just breathe in and out, enjoy the scenery and stay calm. For sure he wasn't going to tell her too much about his family, and she wouldn't be in Zavala Springs long enough to find out on her own. So just roll with it.

As for the kissing-her-senseless part, well, he was too tough to let that bother him for long. He'd been trained as a Ranger, after all. *Hooah!* Steely minded when he wanted to be—or when he was forced to be—this moment had just become one of those times that called for using his dogged determination.

"Josh, I'm guessing you're not currently married," she said quietly from her corner of the seat.

He nearly bit down on his tongue as his steely mind reeled. "What makes you say so?"

"You're not wearing a ring and you said you didn't live anywhere. But that doesn't tell me if you've ever been married, or if you have kids somewhere. Do you?"

Swallowing hard and slowly shaking his head, he answered, "No ex-wife. No children. And it's probably just as well."

"Oh? Why? Don't you like kids?"

The ache in his gut grew into a pain of longing so bad he barely kept from doubling over. He couldn't understand why these old familiar pains hadn't gone away long ago. Geez, you'd think a big, tough guy like him would've gotten over it already.

"Kids are okay, I guess. I've never had a chance to be around them much." He took the opportunity and checked her expression. "What are you getting at?"

From her spot snugged up close to the passenger door, Clare shrugged at Josh's question. "Oh, nothing much." What the devil could she say that didn't make her sound nosy and controlling as hell? "It's only that if you had kids, I would think you'd be much more sympathetic to why I can't take a chance on losing Jimmy."

"I'm plenty sympathetic. I'm taking you two with me and I'm going to help you get away."

She narrowed her lips in a frown to keep herself from asking why. But she decided she had nothing more to add to the conversation. Maybe she'd already said too much.

Josh must have guessed she wanted more information, because he kept trying to explain. "Look. When I said it was probably just as well that I'd never had kids, I was talking about how crazy my life is right now. I got busted out of the Rangers a few months ago and I haven't put my feet back under me yet.

I don't have a job, no house and no ideas of what I want to do next. I have no clue where I'll be for sure next week, let alone six months from now. What kind of life is that for a kid?"

"None." But she also took into consideration the fact that he looked to be about midthirties and he had never been married and didn't seem too interested in having a family anytime soon, if ever.

Clare's slightly shaky—and definitely rattled—mind came to an instant conclusion. As much as this guy was hot and turned her knees to mush when he glanced her way, and as much as he had come to their rescue several times, he was not now nor ever would be the guy for her. She wanted a big family badly. Always had. There would be a lot more children coming into her life, she just knew it. And she needed a steady guy who wanted kids as badly as she did in order to get that family.

Clare wanted a career, too, of course. She wanted it all. But didn't women these days have a chance of getting it all? Gulping down a bubble of indecision mixed with apprehension, she tried to find some semblance of her old backbone. She and Jimmy had come this far. She would find a way out of the mess she'd caused. And then, when they were finally safe, she would also find a nice man who wanted a family. One who wanted to stand shoulder to shoulder with her as they went through life together, working and raising kids. He had to be out there somewhere.

Josh Ryan definitely didn't qualify as the life partner she envisioned.

He guided Lucille onto the Southwest Freeway and within twenty minutes they were miles out of Houston. The fast-food places and convenience store/gas stations gave way to big unbroken parcels of live oak and cottonwood, while the sun came peeking through a patch of early morning haze and lit their surroundings. Daylight. A new day. There had been a time last night when she didn't think she would live to have another day with Jimmy.

Cranking her neck, she glanced over her shoulder to check on the baby. He was still sleeping soundly. She had kept him up too late last night. Chalk one more mistake against her.

Clare let her gaze wander from Jimmy's seat to stare out the back window. Scanning the road behind them, she looked for any sign that someone might be following them. But she saw nothing out of the ordinary in the growing light of dawn. Just the usual early-morning traffic. Relaxing in her seat, she leaned her head back against the headrest. Maybe she could get a few minutes' sleep herself.

When she next opened her eyes, the sun was higher in the sky, pouring heat through the back windshield and raising the temperature in the pickup's cab. Jimmy was making his normal morning waking-up-and-now-it's-time-to-eat noises in the backseat. Clare looked at her watch and was surprised to see it was already nearing nine o'clock. They would have to stop soon for food and a change of diapers.

She glanced out the windshield and noticed a gentle difference in the scenery. They were no longer on a main expressway but were traveling down a back country highway. The landscape and the vegetation passing by weren't quite the same as before. But it didn't look like West Texas scenery, either, the kind she remembered with its parched fields, cedars and hackberries hidden down in gullies and canyons. Instead, the view outside the truck's window was more of a rolling landscape. She did recognize the mesquite, and some scrawny purple sage interspersed between rows of good raw land laid bare for planting. Those things had taken the place of the tall pines, willows and swampland feel of the countryside around Houston.

Clare tried to recall what she'd heard about Zavala Springs. It wasn't much. They area was known for one main thing, the huge Delgado Ranch. One of the largest cattle ranches in the world, the Delgado raised and fed cattle, horses and exotic animals. They also grew oil and gas wells in abundance. The headquarters for the Delgado were located in Zavala Springs. She'd never been there, but her father had gone many times to sell drilling supplies to the Delgado Ranch people.

Clare let her mind wander over old memories of what her dad had told her, and then on to what she'd heard rumored in oil circles. Since she'd been a kid, she had known about the original Spanish land grant for the ranch belonging to a family named Delgado. But about twenty-five years ago, hadn't the last Delgado died and left it to his son-in-law? Now what had been that new owner's name, anyway? With a jolt, she remembered. The son-in-law's name was Ryan.

She jerked her head around to stare at Josh. It would be too much of a coincidence that he came from Zavala Springs and had the last name of Ryan if he didn't belong to the same family that owned the ranch. Drawing in a breath, she stared at his camo pants and beat-up old Stetson, while at the same time listening to the wheezing noises of his fifteen-year-old pickup rumbling beneath her bottom. Clare figured he must be a distant cousin or a black sheep or something. This tough but regular guy just couldn't come from the Delgado wealth.

It wouldn't matter to her one way or the other if he was rich, of course. That wasn't anything she ever noticed about people or really cared about at all. No, wait. She amended that. If Josh was wealthy, it would mean another strike against him. She'd already done the wealthy lover thing once. Oh, yeah. His being one of the Ryans would just seal the deal for her—and not in his favor.

She looked at Josh again and noticed the grim lines set around his mouth. They told the tale of long hours spent behind the wheel, driving straight through the night. Wealthy or not, the man had saved their lives and was continuing to go out of his way to help secure their freedom.

That gave him points in his favor. Enough to make him a

friend in need. But not nearly enough to cause her to change her mind. There wasn't a chance in hell she would ever let herself get romantically involved with Josh, no matter how much being close to him might turn her on.

She stretched her arms and yawned. "Is there anyplace up ahead where we can get coffee and maybe breakfast for the baby?"

Josh started when he heard her voice, but recovered quickly enough and turned to her. "You're awake. Good thing. I've been hearing Jimmy stirring in his car seat.

"And to answer your question, yeah, there's a last-chance convenience store in a few miles and I was going to stop for gas anyway. It'll be the only place to get gas or anything else for the next couple of hours of driving into Zavala Springs."

"What? No stores of any kind for two hours? It can't be that remote in this part of Texas. Not really. Even the vast stretches of nothingness in West Texas don't go on for over two hours of dead driving time."

He slanted a half smile at her. "Ah, but in this part of Texas there's just a few large ranches, and most won't allow any other businesses on their land. The state of Texas is lucky the ranchers let them put public roads through in the middle of the last century. Otherwise, the folks living along the Mexican border might have to pay a toll in order to reach their homes—or go by boat."

Clare tsked at the very idea. But then she stopped, biting down on her lip at the very real fact of such open and remote space and of the enormously wealthy families who controlled all the land.

Josh finished pumping the gas while Clare stood beside the truck, bending over to change Jimmy's diaper as he lay in the front seat. When that was done, she pulled a clean T-shirt over the baby's head.

Turning from the sight of the sexy mother leaning over her child, Josh took a deep breath to clear his mind. The air here was drier than it had been in Houston, and full of the hay and sage smells like he remembered from when he grew up in these parts. He hadn't been home in nearly fourteen years, and he wasn't particularly happy about going there now.

Well, that wasn't strictly the whole truth. He was happy for the chance to see his sister again. It had been much too long since that time she'd come to visit him in the hospital when he'd first returned to the States from the "'Stan." Josh hadn't been all that glad to see her then, as he thought about it now. But bless Maggie, she never took offense at his ornery moods. Guess that was due to her occasionally having a few blue moods herself.

God, he'd been missing her. And his brother, Ethan, too. And Grandpa Will. Ah, Grandpa Will. Seemed like you never knew how much someone meant to you until it was too late.

Josh heaved a heavy sigh. He could scarcely believe there would never be another opportunity to visit with his grandfather, Will Ryan. It didn't seem possible that his father's father could really be gone for good. It made Josh think of his own mortality, and that did nothing to help his melancholy.

One more arrow of guilt punctured Josh's heart. He'd never made it back to tell the only grandfather he could remember how much he meant to him. Or how much Josh appreciated it when his grandfather and grandmother stepped up and took in Maggie when their mother died.

After their mother had been killed in that freak plane accident, Josh had thought their father should've been the one to step in and become both father and mother for his own teenage children—especially fifteen-year-old Maggie. But the mighty Brody Ryan would never bend enough to become a real parent. It was one of those memories from his past that Josh had never settled in his mind. One of the many things he'd wanted time alone to consider.

"Okay, we're ready to eat now if you are," Clare picked up

her son and turned to face him. "I could sure use a hot shower and Jimmy needs a bath in the worst way. But I guess we're presentable enough to go for fast-food."

Josh supposed his alone time would just have to wait. "Why don't you go on over and get in line while I move the truck away from the pumps."

A half hour later, they were fed and Jimmy had been allowed a few free moments to toddle around in the restaurant's indoor playground under his mother's hawkish gaze. Back outside beside the truck, Josh stood against the open door next to Clare while she tried to ease Jimmy into the car seat. No luck.

"Anything I can do?" he asked as she pulled her boy back out of the pickup and began speaking to him in a soft but stern tone.

She shot Josh a quick "don't interfere" glance and then turned her attention back to Jimmy. "Please do what I say, honey. Your mama needs you to be a good boy and help her out. We have to work together here."

Jimmy wasn't having any of it. "No!"

Clare's patience at first seemed endless as she tried cajoling and then bribing her child. She was everything he ever remembered about a mother. Josh had to hold back his smile before it threatened to undo what she was trying to accomplish with her son. The woman was something else. She reminded him of his own mama. Strong-willed, firm but loving and unendingly patient with her child.

Maggie was going to love her.

After standing around in the hot Texas sun for a full ten minutes, biding time while Clare fought to get Jimmy settled down, Josh couldn't wait any longer. He eased around Clare's body and pulled Jimmy from her arms before either the mama or the boy knew what had happened.

"*Heyuuup*, boy," he snapped in his best drill sergeant's cadence as he swung the kid around and dropped him into the seat. "*A—tennn—shun!*"

Jimmy gaped up at him with his mouth wide-open and easily slid down into his seat with no fuss. Guess even a baby recognized authority when he heard it.

"You pay attention when your mama speaks," Josh said firmly as he locked the kid into the restraints. "There you go."

When Josh turned back around, Clare was glaring at him. Uh-oh. Had he overstepped some boundary without thinking and made her angry? He knew her well enough by now to see that she wanted to feel in charge of the parenting duties with her own son, and he admired her for it. But, hell, there came a time when enough was enough.

"I'm sorry if I did anything…" He stopped talking and stared down into that beautiful face, captivated by the tiny glint he caught in her eyes.

The first real sign she wasn't mad came as the corners of both her eyes and mouth crinkled up. Pretty soon she was smiling at him with what turned into a full grin.

Josh couldn't remember the last time he'd really smiled all out. His sense of humor had been AWOL for months—years, maybe. But when he looked at her mouth turned up in that wide smile, he found himself grinning back. He was fascinated by her mouth.

"Thank you," she said with a flirtatious giggle in her voice.

Without thinking, only needing to feel her warmth, he leaned in closer. "I…uh…don't know what to say," he murmured. He was hovering within an inch of those tantalizing lips, caught between a wish and a prayer.

"Say, 'You're welcome.'"

The soft whisper of air from her words fanned over his face as he closed his eyes and breathed her in. What would she do if he narrowed the gap between their lips and bent for a taste of those luscious lips?

He reached out and ended up grabbing a handful of air.

The slam of Lucille's front passenger door behind him told him everything he needed to know about what she would or would not do. Hot damn. He should've known better.

Chapter 4

Not ready to discuss their almost-kiss, Clare spent the next two hours finding ways to divert Jimmy's attention from the long, boring ride. She handed the baby one of his favorite soft blocks, then a handful of fish crackers and finally told him a story he loved hearing over and over.

She'd been willing to do anything to keep Jimmy's mind off getting out of his car seat to play—and her mind off Josh. Lucille's cab had suddenly become too small by a factor of one very broad-shouldered man. But Josh didn't seem to be facing the same problems she and Jimmy were. After nearly driving her mad with those intense looks and lust-filled expressions, he now drove the narrowing roads stoically and paid no attention to either one of them.

He'd been good with Jimmy at the gas stop. So good it had almost made her cry. The baby also noticed his firm but gentle care, and occasionally looked up at the back of his head with obvious admiration and yearning. Jimmy had never reacted with such instant bonding to any man, not even his own father. But then Ramzi was always too busy to pay much attention. In Ramzi's world, babies were consigned to the women's domain until old enough to be educated.

Josh had somehow known just what to do to settle and soothe her boy. She had been sorely tempted to find out how good Josh could be with her, too. As he'd stood beside her by the truck, she'd been suddenly wild with need. Narrowing the tiny gap that he'd infuriatingly left between them in a desperate attempt for just one taste had become an instant and insistent obsession. One she had fought hard to conquer, and congratulated herself for having mastered when she'd finally stepped away.

What was with her? She'd known the man less than a day. Furthermore, she had promised herself there would not be any romantic involvement with someone so obviously uninterested in making a commitment to a family.

Was Josh really not interested in kids? What about those longing looks he had given Jimmy? She knew what she'd been seeing. Those were the same kind of wistful looks she knew had been in her own eyes for babies before Jimmy was born. The damn man was confusing as hell with his gentleness and—and his declarations of not caring.

It was enough to make her wish for more time to figure him out. But her main concern, the entire focus of her existence for the immediate future, had to be finding a way to keep Ramzi from taking Jimmy back to Abu Fujarah.

Sighing in frustration, she sat back in her seat just as they drove past the sign that said Welcome To Zavala Springs. Except for a sleek new office complex built outside the old part of the town proper, the place didn't look too different from any small town. Beyond the new-looking complex, they passed two brand-new multistory hotels and a couple of national chain restaurants. The newness of everything made the area look prosperous.

"Do those new buildings we passed just inside the town limits belong to the Delgado Ranch?" she asked Josh.

He shrugged a shoulder. "Beats me. I haven't been back in a lot of years. But I'd have to guess they do. I can't imagine any other businesses would make that kind of investment in Zavala Springs…or that the Delgado would allow anyone else to buy that much land from the company."

"Does all the land in town belong to the Delgado, too?" She hadn't thought of that, but it seemed logical when she considered how big and powerful the ranch and its owners were.

"Most of the land for a fifty-mile radius is part of the company's holdings. Zavala Springs started out as a company town. I'd guess you could say it was sort of an expanded bunkhouse for the families of the ranch hands and those who worked at the wells. When the ranch last changed hands a couple of decades ago, many of the employees' families inherited the land where they had been working or residing."

"You mean the last actual owner named Delgado left parts of the town to the citizens in his will? As sort of a reward?"

"Yes, ma'am. That's just the way it was."

Wanting to ask him how he was related to the Ryans and the Delgados but afraid she would sound either nosy or pushy, Clare left their conversation at that and stared out the window. The town was neat and clean, even though the mostly one-story stucco and shingled buildings on the main street didn't look exactly new. She imagined that the whole place was probably no more than a hundred years old at most, but it still seemed to belong to another time. Small live oaks grew in planting beds next to the sidewalks, and there were colorful flowers in pots at every corner.

Certainly Ramzi's men could never follow them here. Clare took her first real easy breath of air since she'd left Abu Fujarah.

On the other side of the small town's business district, Josh turned the pickup down a side street. Here the trees were taller, and though there were no sidewalks, houses set on grass lawns and painted in soft pastel colors lined the street on both sides.

"Where are we headed?"

"My grandfather Will lives...lived...in a big house in town for as long as I can remember. And my younger sister has been living there with him since our mother died back when we were teens. My guess is she's going to stay on now that he's gone, but I haven't had a chance to talk to her about her plans."

His mother was dead. It hadn't occurred to Clare to ask about his immediate family. His parents. His siblings. Wouldn't that be one way to find out if he was related to the Ryans of the Delgado Ranch?

"What's your sister's name? And does she have any kids?"

Josh's lips quirked up in something that resembled a smile. "Her name is Maggie. She's never been married and has never had babies. But she loves them. Her best friend is the next-door neighbor who has a youngster of her own and runs a day care out of her home. Maggie is over there a lot." Josh threw a glance back at Jimmy. "Maggie is really going to enjoy having your son in the house."

"She doesn't know we're coming, does she? Are you sure it's going to be okay to have us come barging in on her when her grandfather just died?"

"It'll be fine. Wait and see."

In a small office right off the lobby of the Abu Fujarah Embassy in Washington, Abdullah Ramzi al-Hamzah questioned the man he had hired to find his son. "So your employees actually had my son within their reach in Houston but let his mother spirit him away? That is not the result I'm paying a small fortune to achieve. How did it go wrong?"

"That we found them at all was no small feat, Excellency. The American woman apparently has confederates here in her homeland that are helping to keep your child hidden. But there is nowhere she can hide the child for long. I have hired new men, men more familiar with the country who are new-technology experts. We are watching anyone who has ever come in contact with her and we will find her. It's only a question of hours, perhaps a few days at most."

Ramzi fisted his hands but stuck them in his pockets. He was frustrated beyond belief. His child. His beloved son. Taken from his place of birth and from the bosom of his rightful family.

Clare. Ramzi never imagined such a beautiful and gracious woman would be capable of committing the treachery of stealing his only son. At the end of their marriage, she had ceased to mean anything in his life. A minor annoyance only. He had been prepared never to think of her again once she was banished from his country. Now, he could think of nothing else.

"I will give you another forty-eight hours," he told his employee. "Though I charge you to remember my instructions. I care nothing for what happens to the woman but my son is not to be put in danger. If baby Prince Bashshar is harmed in any way, I will hold you responsible.

"In the meantime," Ramzi continued, "our diplomats are in the midst of negotiations with the U.S. State Department. I want no possibility of that woman seeking the help of her government in order to keep my child from his home. The U.S. must learn that harboring her will cause a serious rift in our oil negotiations. Soon she will be a fugitive in her own country. Neither friends nor any allies will give her refuge legally."

Ramzi willed his temper back in place. He had to keep his mind focused on the goal. The return of his son. There would be time enough afterward to think of consequences.

* * *

Josh pulled the truck up in front of his grandfather's home and was surprised to find a small asphalt parking area had been built beside the house. He'd almost forgotten that Grandpa Will had been running his private investigator's business out of his home. The memories he'd kept in his heart were of his grandfather being a cop, but that had been long ago. It made Josh suddenly wonder what would happen to the P.I. business now that Grandpa Will was gone.

"This is it? What a cool place." Clare sat and stared out the window for a few seconds. "You're sure…"

"Come on. You take care of Jimmy. I'll tote the stuff."

The house looked like something out of a book, Josh thought idly as he gathered up their things. But he'd never thought about that while growing up. It had just been the place where his father's second-generation Irish parents had lived. Now, looking up at the three stories with their gingerbread facade and at the wide porch encircling the entire house, he figured his grandfather's home could possibly be considered cool, if you looked at it with fresh sight.

It could also be considered slightly run-down, as Josh noticed when he helped Clare and Jimmy up the front porch steps. The peeling paint and the worn boards of the steps spoke of neglect. While his grandmother Fiona had been alive, this place had never looked shabby. But she'd been gone a long time now. She'd passed away right after Maggie had graduated from college, about eight years ago.

Josh was sort of surprised that Maggie hadn't been helping out with keeping the place up. She'd always been a whiz with tools. Maybe she'd had her hands full lately. If he decided to hang around a while after the funeral—and after he found a way to help Clare—he'd offer to fix a few things up around the old place. It would give him time to think.

He knocked on the door to his grandfather's house, which was a first. He'd never even thought of knocking when his grandmother and grandfather had been alive. But it had been so long since he'd been home. And they were both gone now. He just didn't feel comfortable here anymore.

After a moment or two, and there still was no answer, he knocked harder.

"Does your sister have a job?" Clare asked. "Maybe she's gone shopping or to work or something and isn't at home. We should've called when we stopped for gas."

"Maggie's been helping out with the business my grandfather ran from his home. If my sister is working, she'll be here and should hear the front door. But you're right, she could be out shopping. Somehow I can't really imagine Maggie would be working on the day before Granddad's funeral." He tried the door and found it open.

Stepping into the front hall, Josh called out, "Hey, Maggie girl. It's your brother. Where are you?" He pulled Clare and Jimmy inside the house behind him and shut the front door.

Clare tried to look in all directions at once. There were plants everywhere, resting on every surface and hanging in baskets strung from shelves and by corner brackets. And here and there amongst all the greenery, candles were burning and giving off the most wondrous scents. The place smelled earthy and sensual. Homey. Magical.

A female voice came from somewhere nearby. "I'm coming. For heaven's sake quit your…" The voice trailed off as the young woman appeared in a doorway. "Oh."

She stopped midstep, staring at Jimmy, who was quiet in Clare's arms. "Oh. Oh my." Without taking her eyes off the baby, she spoke to Josh. "I figured you'd be coming in today, brother, but I didn't know you'd be bringing…friends."

Josh set their stuff down on the floor as he captured his sister in his arms. "Come here, sugar, and give your big brother a hug. I've missed you, Maggie."

Clare watched as Josh swung the young woman around in a tight circle. From what she'd seen so far, his sister was a tiny woman who appeared to be about thirty, and stood about three or four inches shorter than Clare's own five-seven. With a compact body, Maggie's lean frame looked almost muscular, yet she was definitely feminine at the same time. She had an exotic look, with a vanilla-caramel complexion and dark auburn hair—and maybe the most beautiful green eyes Clare had ever seen. The overall effect made for quite a picture.

And so did the sight of the two grown-ups dancing around the room. Jimmy got caught up in Josh's playfulness. Her little boy pointed a finger at the adult brother and sister duo acting silly and shrieked with glee. He rocked in Clare's arms and tried to make her let him loose, obviously wanting to join in the fun.

"Hold on, honey. It's not your time yet. I'll play with you in a minute." Clare's heart ached for her son, wishing that he had a brother or sister who would find such joy with him. Oh, he did have half sisters back in Abu Fujarah. But she had never seen any of them actually playing. They'd always seemed so serious, and not just a little suspicious of their American half brother. Stand-offish and wary, they had never asked to see or hold him. Clare's smile slipped some at the thought and her eyes grew watery.

Maggie finally broke free of her brother's embrace and socked the big guy on the arm. "Where are your manners? Introduce us."

Josh caught his breath and grinned down at his sister before glancing over to where Clare was standing. "Sorry. Clare and Jimmy Chandler, I would like for you to meet my sister, Margarita Elena Inez Delgado Ryan. Maggie to everyone who loves her. And most people do. To the few left on earth that don't know her, she's Ms. Ryan."

Maggie beamed over at Clare before she knuckled her brother in the arm again.

"Ow," Josh said, feigning real pain at the spot where he'd been hit. "I take that back. Not *everyone* loves her."

"Shut up, Josh," Maggie said as she kept her eyes trained on Jimmy. "Let me get acquainted with your friends."

It didn't take Jimmy long to make a decision about this stranger. The baby held out his arms to her and let it be known he was ready to get closer and make a new friend.

Maggie took her eyes off Jimmy long enough to ask Clare, "Would it be okay if I held him?" She held out her arms and Jimmy literally jumped a full foot to land in them.

"Well, I guess what I think doesn't matter," Clare said with a chuckle. Both Maggie and Clare laughed as the baby looked up to the new woman holding him and grinned.

He clapped his hands and giggled. "Down."

"Not just yet, baby." Maggie tickled his tummy and Jimmy squealed in delight.

Clare immediately decided she liked Josh's sister. "I hope we won't be in your way. Josh said you wouldn't mind taking us in until we can think of what we need to do next, but I don't want you to go to any trouble."

A glimmer sparked in Maggie's eyes. "You mean I get to keep you two for a while? I can't think of anything I'd like better. You know how to cook?"

The surprising question startled Clare, but she recovered in a hurry. She had a feeling she would need to be quick to keep up with this ball of fire. "Some. I'm not a gourmet or anything but…"

"Good enough. I've been working on the spread for Grand-dad's wake and I could sure use some help."

Josh stepped to Clare's side, interrupting the easy flow between her and Maggie. "Clare didn't come here to help us, Mags. She's the one needs the help. Just give her a chance—"

Clare put her hand on his chest to stop him from saying any more. "Could we explain it all later? Both Jimmy and I need a bath and a change of clothes."

Before she could move away, Josh put his hand down and captured hers where it lay over his beating heart. He stared down, sober and concerned, and his gaze searched her eyes for some sign he was obviously hoping to see. Immediate awareness of his heat, his heartbeat and the disturbing sensation they caused in the small of her back all raised goose bumps on her skin.

God, what was she thinking, to come to this man's family home? A home meant intimacy...bathing arrangements...and sleeping arrangements. Things that hadn't been a problem while they were on the road. Clare eased her hand out from under his and finally caught her breath again.

"Geez. I accused Josh of forgetting his manners, and just look how I did the same." Maggie used her free hand to touch Clare's shoulder. "You do look all done in. Come on upstairs with me and I'll show you where everything is.

"Meanwhile," she added over her shoulder as she turned and headed toward the stairs, "Josh will bring your things up and then he'll be glad to help me out in the kitchen. Won't you, brother?"

Josh grunted, then leaned down for their bags. "KP isn't exactly my strong suit," he mumbled.

Clare hid her chuckle as Maggie totally ignored him and led the way upstairs.

"You want to give me a hint why you would bring a total stranger and a baby here on the day before our grandfather's funeral?" Maggie was standing in the kitchen whispering at the top of her lungs.

Josh shrugged. "She's got problems. I couldn't just leave her stranded by the side of the road, could I?"

"I don't know. Tell me what her problem is and then I can

make my own decision." Maggie picked up a chopping knife and went to work on the vegetables she'd set on the counter earlier.

"Why don't we wait for Ethan. Then she'll only have to tell her story once."

"She's running from trouble, isn't she?" Maggie waved the knife around in the air like a wand. "Is it the cops?"

"Does she seem like the type to be wanted by the law?" he asked grudgingly. "She's running, but it's from her ex. Let her tell her own story when Ethan gets here."

Josh went to the counter, picked up a jalapeño pepper by its stem and bit the entire thing off whole the way he'd done all his life. "Anyway," he began again after he swallowed the heat, "you like her. I saw the look on your face when the two of you were talking. You aren't about to kick her out without giving her a chance. And besides, I know you're already crazy about Jimmy. You were jonesing on the kid within thirty seconds of seeing him."

"You know how I feel about kids."

Josh nodded, but couldn't bring himself to talk about her feelings or anything else to do with children. The whole subject was still too sore, like a festering splinter stuck under the skin that couldn't be worked out.

Maggie turned, still holding her knife but lost in thought. "Where are they going to sleep? I can put them into Granddad's old room, it's the biggest. But that boy needs his own small bed. Maybe not a crib exactly, he's too big for that. But a bed his own size."

"Can we borrow one from your buddy Larado next door?"

She shook her head. "The one she's got is in constant use. I'm sure Lara couldn't spare it. But…" Maggie suddenly stopped speaking and nodded as if she'd just figured something out. "Of course. There's Mom's old toddler bed. You remember. I think you used it, too, when you were small. It's the one cut from mesquite logs that a ranch hand made for her when she was a baby. Why don't you go pick it up and bring it here?"

"I remember. Where is it?"

"The last time I saw it was in the attic out at the old Delgado homestead."

"At Abuela Lupe's?" An automatic chill rode down his spine. "I don't know.… Has anyone been there since she went back to her mother's in Mexico?"

"I've been there lots of times over the last fourteen-plus years. When she left, Abuela Lupe said the house belongs to us kids as much as to her." Maggie narrowed her eyes at him. "I'm not too crazy about the way you said Abuela 'went back'—like she had a choice. What's happened to you, Josh? You used to call things as you saw them. Our grandmother Lupe didn't go back to Mexico of her own free will, and you know it. I'd appreciate it if you wouldn't talk now like it was somehow her idea."

"Mags, don't start. Not on the eve of Granddad Will's funeral. You don't know how it was. I went along with Dad to Mexico to make sure Abuela was all right. I've told you over and over…"

Maggie waved the knife again and returned to the vegetables. "Just go get the baby bed. You're right. This is no time to talk about it, not with Clare and Jimmy here."

It occurred to him then that he might not be smart to leave his sister alone with Clare. "I'll go. But first promise me you won't tell Clare about…about us."

Maggie swung on him with her lips tightened down in a scowl as she stood toe-to-toe with him. "You mean you don't want your new girlfriend to know about us being *special?* How very civilized and dishonest of you, brother."

"She's not my girlfriend." He ground his teeth, wishing deep inside that he could have some kind of chance with Clare. But there was no possibility.

"Look," he said after he'd pried his jaw apart. "The magic Abuela Lupe taught us years ago was only kid stuff. We were just teenagers, not ready for the really heavy spells and potions. And

I haven't used any of it. Not once since I left home." The very thought made his skin crawl.

"Well, I have." Maggie glared at him. "Ethan does, too, sometimes. We both wish we'd had time to learn a lot more."

"I don't want to know about what the two of you do or do not use," Josh said between gritted teeth. "And I sure as hell don't want Clare to know. Promise, or we're leaving here right now."

Maggie frowned again, but finally took a deep breath. "All right. I promise. But not talking about it doesn't make it go away. We are what we are."

Roger that. Having descended from witches. How frigging *special*.

Chapter 5

Every fence post on the road to the old Delgado homestead took Josh back. He'd ridden this fence line so many times over the years, he knew every strand of wire. On the cool early mornings and through the hot, dry dusks of his childhood, he and ol' Molly had plowed through the sagebrush dodging rattlesnakes to check on these same posts and wire. By the age of nine, he remembered riding Molly out this way to join the other hands with the spring sorting and branding taking place right over that hill in the Delgado Creek corral.

But it was the teenage years, before his mother died, that he remembered best. Those times when he would give his horse her head and race across the range, full of piss and vinegar and ready to explode with hormones blazing. Every season had a scent of its own then. Summers smelled of freedom, raw and wild, and brought to mind extreme heat and a range grown thick with prickly pear. Fall's smell was more subdued, with hay and tall grasses filling his nostrils as he rode the range with whatever fresh young girl had been a current favorite. The winter had smelled crisp and clean then, with a hint of wood smoke and a touch of reckless-ness. But it was the newer scents of the spring that lingered in his mind. Spring smelled of rebirth and budding futures. That time when the world was his, the possibilities endless.

When Josh last rode Molly over this range it had been spring, too. Full of pain, grief and anger, he'd blindly galloped across the fields and creek beds, trying to leave behind his thoughts. It hadn't worked. No matter what he'd done or where he'd gone, his mind couldn't shake the dark traumas and dreaded magic. Those same nightmares continued chasing him after he'd left the Delgado for good. They'd stuck with him through the years. In truth, still deviled him today.

By the time Josh drove Lucille into the yard of the old Delgado homestead, his mind roiled with turmoil. Coming here was bound to be a mistake. Throughout his life he'd usually found ways of brushing aside the pain of his mother's death and those traumas that had come afterward. The many years he'd been gone from the Delgado had helped ease the strong ache of losing his mom, but he had never forgotten the circumstances. And he had never been able to completely bury his guilt or the anger.

Pulling the key from his pocket, Josh climbed out of Lucille and stalked toward the wide front porch of his ancestors' home, still convinced this was a bad idea. In all the house's nearly two hundred years of standing here in the midst of a copse of pecans and ebony, there had never been need for a key. But then the place had never been left empty this long, either. Maggie said there had been some trouble with squatters over the last few years, mostly drug smugglers coming across the border in need of water and shelter. That was as good a reason as any for strong locks. Anyone was welcome to the water in the well, as that would be a matter of life and death. But no one broke into a Delgado structure.

Josh stood frozen at the threshold with his shaky hand on the knob, unable to turn the key as he tried to put aside his raging emotions. He'd be no help for Clare and Jimmy if he couldn't get himself together any better than this. But of course, he'd known coming back to Abuela Lupe's house would be bad. He just hadn't known how bad.

Right then another rotten thought hit him. What if his father planned on attending Granddad Will's funeral tomorrow? Hey, that was a stupid thought. Of course his old man would be at his own father's funeral. The two Ryan men hadn't gotten along real well over the years, but Josh knew each of them believed family counted for everything.

Jeez. Could he manage to attend his beloved grandfather's funeral and actually have to face his father on the same day without hitting something—or someone?

Josh drew in a deep breath and shoved aside the worst of his shakes. He was a Ranger. He could face anything that didn't depend on him making decisions about someone else's life, despite what the shrinks in the military said.

Walking through the house wasn't as bad as he'd expected. Yes, the place was filled with memories. But these memories were all of happy times. Passing by the empty antique rifle cabinets, he thought back to hunting trips with his father and brother in better times. He spotted the old rough-hewn furniture and his grandmother's many ceramic pots and crystals, sitting on every shelf and table. They made him remember Abuela Lupe's gentle ways.

At last, Josh climbed the stairs to the attic and without any trouble found the child's bed he'd promised to locate. The bed had been stored in three pieces and should be easy enough to carry out to the truck.

On his third trip down the stairs, he heard a noise. Standing stock-still on the staircase, Josh held his breath and listened.

Someone had driven into the yard outside and was walking up the front porch stairs with heavy-booted steps.

Damn. Why didn't he have a rifle with him? And why hadn't he locked the door behind himself when he'd gone in and out?

The front door banged open. "Joshua? Where are you, son?"

Holy crap. That was his father's voice. He recognized it easily enough, as though the last fourteen years had never happened. What the hell was Brody Ryan doing here?

Well, it looked like Josh was going to find out what would happen when he came face-to-face with his father—sooner rather than later.

"I'm up here," he called out. "On the way downstairs."

Another minute and the two generations of Ryan men stood staring each other down.

Josh broke the tension-filled silence first. "How'd you know I was here?"

"Nobody drives down a Delgado Ranch road without people noticing," his father said with a nod. "Plus, we always keep men watching this old homestead. I gave your grandmother Lupe my oath the place wouldn't come to any harm."

Josh wondered at the words, so easily spoken. As though his father's oath, especially given to Abuela Lupe, meant anything at all. Lifting his chin, he set his jaw and looked his father in the eye, glad his hands were full of baby bed pieces at the moment.

"But why did the great Brody Ryan himself need to do the checking?" he spat out in disgust. "Don't you have plenty of hands who could've—"

"It's no secret you've come home for your grandfather's funeral," Brody cut in sternly. "And who else would be driving that shameful broken-down old truck parked out there? Still calling it 'Lucille' like it's some kind of girlfriend?

"I wanted to see you," his father added in a firmer tone.

"But why bother coming all the way out here?" Josh had to force the whine out of his voice. "You'll see me tomorrow at the funeral."

His father's narrowed eyes scrutinized him. "What I see is that you're still running from the truth after all these years."

Trust his father to cut to the core of the matter. But Josh had no intention of rehashing old problems with him. He couldn't even manage to be civil to the man right now.

"I've tried talking to you many times," Brody told him without waiting for Josh to say anything. "I even flew over to that god-forsaken base where you were stationed in that godforsaken and isolated country, all in an effort to get you to talk to me. But every time I've reached out, you've refused. This isolated old house is as good a place as any to make you listen."

Josh shoved past his father and headed for the front door. "Sorry. I've heard it all before. Not interested."

"Josh. Your mother's death was an accident. I hadn't been drinking at that party. I swear. I don't drink and fly airplanes. Not then. Not now. Not ever."

Swinging back to face his old man, Josh groaned under his breath. "Tell it to someone who cares. Like Abuela Lupe, for instance."

"I tried to talk to my mother-in-law fifteen years ago, right after the crash," Brody said with force. "You know that. And you know how spooky-odd Lupe got then. At the time, as I recall, you didn't think it was wrong for your Abuela Lupe to go back to Mexico. You even came with us. You must remember, your grandmother just went kind of nuts when her only daughter died, accusing me of all kinds of wrongs. There was no settling her down or talking to her.

"And no talking to her even crazier mother back in Mexico, either," Brody added with a sigh. "Both of those weird old women should be committed."

Unfortunately, Josh remembered his grandmother's tears and

his great-grandmother's words all too clearly. "So you don't believe Abuela Lupe's mother is really a witch with the power to put curses on people?"

"Of course not. Though it looks like she was right when she predicted my children would leave the Delgado and me behind for good."

That hadn't been a part of the curse, Josh remembered.

The ancient woman's words rang clear in his ears to this day. She'd issued her curse and then gone on to say, "You son of a dog! You've murdered my grandchild and banished my child. Your children will leave your house with hatred in their hearts toward the man who took their mother and grandmother away. You deserve this punishment and are bound to suffer for your sins. All of you will suffer for the sins of the father. *Vete pa'l carajo!* Go to hell."

Josh shook his head free of the memory and flexed his muscles under the heavy load. "Talking about this does no good. Not after all this time. Your own father has just passed away. Doesn't that mean anything to you?"

"Dad was sick for a long while," Brody said more softly than Josh had ever heard him speak. "I didn't want him to suffer. So yes, his going means a lot. But my children are very much alive. You're alive, boy. Despite your efforts to bring yourself to a flashing end in the Rangers."

The flame of anger that usually simmered right beneath the surface suddenly burned quick and bright in Josh's heart. "You don't know what you're saying. I'm outta here." He spun around and stormed toward the front door, leaving before it was too late to catch the rest of the spiteful words clogged in his throat.

"I just want to help you, Josh," his father called out from behind him.

Without another word and without turning back, Josh threw the rest of the furniture pieces into the pickup's bed and roared off, throwing a cloud of caliche dust in his wake.

He'd been trying to bury those memories of his mother's death and the old witch's curse for years. Now after one quick trip down memory lane with his father, he would have to start forcing them into his subconscious all over again.

Damn. Damn. Damn.

Evening settled over the town of Zavala Springs, bringing a lavender haze to the land and rose-colored streaks across the cobalt sky. Clare brushed Jimmy's baby-fine hair back from his face and hefted him up on her hip for the trip downstairs to Maggie's kitchen. At least at this point they were both clean and somewhat rested.

Maggie had come upstairs hours ago to say Josh had gone out to pick up a baby bed. But Clare had been listening and hadn't heard anything that sounded like Josh's return. Would it take almost three hours to run his errand? The distances here in Texas were far greater than most people realized. So she would have to guess it was possible. But she didn't like being without him for this long.

Her foot almost slipped against the stair and she stopped to catch her breath. Since when had Josh's presence become so important in her life? And why did she feel like she might die if he didn't return right now?

Yes, he had saved them. Yes, he had turned out to be kind underneath all the irritable grunts and disclaimers. And hell yes, she wanted to give in to the special kind of anticipation she felt when he gave her one of those intense stares.

But being struck by such a powerful need for any man was so not like her. She didn't do flings and didn't believe in love at first sight. She hardly believed in love at all anymore. At least not the way she had once upon a time.

Yet this sudden obsession to get to know him better, both physically and emotionally, had begun to consume her thoughts and apparently her subconscious. Her yearnings for Josh were far different than she'd ever felt before, and nowhere near what they had been with Ramzi. But she wasn't sure exactly why.

She could imagine how things would be with him, though. How it would be to lie down beside him. What it would be like to have those strong, work-roughened hands on her skin. The way it would be to take him inside, to enfold him into her body and into her heart.

Jimmy began to squirm on her hip and Clare remembered they'd been headed down to find him something to eat. "Okay, sweet pea. Mama's done daydreaming about stuff that can't happen. Sorry for the delay. Let's go get you that cracker like I promised."

They found Maggie in her kitchen just as a loud knock sounded at the back door. Automatically they all turned to see a nicely dressed man stick his head inside the room.

"Hey, sis. Did I make it in time for supper?" The man was tall, hard-edged and movie-star handsome. Obviously related to Maggie and Josh, this Ryan had dark curly hair, a pretty-boy face and shoulders broad enough to take on the world. A little too slick in Clare's opinion, but sexy enough to leave broken hearts in every town.

When he stepped into the kitchen and spotted her and Jimmy, his face broke into a wide, disarming grin. Yeah, this one could be a real heartbreaker. Clare preferred Josh's expressive face and gorgeous espresso eyes to his brother's perfect teeth and hair and those steely gray eyes that paid close attention to every single thing in the room. A quick look at the man was like your first glimpse of a huge ice-cream sundae. Beautiful and tempting, but way too many calories to indulge yourself.

"Ethan!" Maggie ran to him and threw her arms around his waist. "I'm so glad to see you, brother."

In contrast to Josh's exuberant greeting, Ethan kissed his sister on the forehead and hugged her tight. It gave Clare a moment more to check him out. Dressed in a charcoal-gray suit with a white shirt and a conservative red-striped tie, this brother just seemed to shout law enforcement. She would bet he would turn out to be an FBI agent or with the U.S. Marshals office, or perhaps a detective for some special high-powered international government unit. In her worldwide travels for the magazine, she'd run into them all.

Maggie stepped back from him and turned to her. "Ethan, meet Josh's friends, Clare Chandler and her son, Jimmy."

Ethan took the few steps toward her with an outstretched arm. "Nice to meet any friend of my brother's." He shook her hand then turned to Jimmy with that big, wide smile turned up on full wattage. "Hey there, boy. Can you shake my hand, too?"

Jimmy clamped his mouth shut, buried his face against his mother's shoulder and threw his arms around her neck. Instead of his usual "No!" he made a low-pitched sound of distress deep in his throat.

Clare patted her son's back absently and tried to make amends. "Sorry. Jimmy's been through a lot in the last few days. He's probably getting cranky. He'll come around. Just give him some time."

"It's okay," Ethan said softly. "Maybe I scared him. I haven't been around kids in a long time. He can take all the time he needs. In this family, kids are number one."

"Oh?" That seemed an odd thing for a man to say about a family that didn't seem to have even one child among them.

As she stood half hidden behind her brother, Maggie cringed. Josh would absolutely freak out if Ethan spilled his guts to Clare about the magic. Rather than panic, Maggie decided to take charge.

Before the other woman could ask the questions obviously gathering behind her eyes, Maggie broke into the tense silence to address her brother. "We're waiting for Josh to get back so

Clare can explain what kind of help she needs, Ethan. Why don't you take your bag upstairs and get changed for—"

"Help?"

"She's only going to tell it once, bubba. After we've all eaten supper. Now go—"

The kitchen door banged open and Josh stepped into the room. "Ethan. I thought that must be your ride out back." Her older brother stepped to Ethan's side and the two gave each other an awkward bear hug, the way men do when they're close but haven't seen each other in a long time.

Maggie's eyes swam at the sight of the two people she loved most trying to find something to say to each other. They'd been inseparable as kids and yet they hadn't seen each other in over fourteen years. It was a pitiful shame.

After they broke apart, Josh put his hand on Ethan's shoulder. "You're not dressed for it, but I could sure use your help getting the old Delgado family baby bed out of my pickup, and then dragging the thing upstairs and putting it back together. Wanna go change?"

Ethan blinked once, and Maggie was afraid of what he might say. But in a second, her middle brother pulled through like he always had in the past.

"Nah. Just let me take off the jacket and tie, then I'm game." Ethan shrugged out of his coat and ripped at the knot in his tie.

"Don't take forever, guys," Maggie said with relief alive in her gut. "Supper is almost ready."

"Hey, you're talking to the two Incredible Hulks here, remember?" Ethan grinned and his eyes sparkled while mentioning the TV character the two brothers had played at emulating as youngsters. At the time, Maggie had been too much into horses and small critters for make-believe.

Both men clomped out of the kitchen together and slammed the door behind them, leaving her standing there with Clare and Jimmy. The baby started to fuss in the sudden silence.

Going to the refrigerator, Maggie poured milk into a plastic cup and then reached for the graham crackers she always kept in the cupboard. "Let me fix him a little something to eat," she told Clare. "We'll serve the supper casserole when the guys get done. Do you think Jimmy will eat what we do?"

Maggie hoped a discussion of the food and the baby's eating preferences would take Clare's mind off Ethan's earlier offhand remark. But she had a feeling her life wasn't going to be that simple.

A half hour later Josh left his brother upstairs to clean up and headed down the stairs. It was great seeing Ethan again after all these years. Josh just wished the circumstances were less traumatic. All of Will Ryan's grandchildren needed to get over their estrangement and the reasons for their separation long enough to help each other get through this time of grief.

And as much as Josh felt the need to help them, he also wished that Clare and Jimmy weren't such a big distraction. He had so much baggage in his background to work through and he'd hoped his brother and sister would be there for him, too....

As he approached the kitchen door he overheard Maggie saying something about children. Slowing down, he decided not to step into the middle of anything potentially hazardous until he could get a feel for what she and Clare were discussing. He eased to a stop beside the door.

"I don't know what I'd do without Jimmy," he heard Clare say. "I'd been waiting to be a mom for my whole life and now I've finally got my chance."

"You do make a good mother," Maggie said soothingly.

"You really think so?"

"Definitely. I work part-time at the day care next door and I see all kinds. You seem like one of the best."

"I hope so." Clare's voice held a wistful tone. "It's my greatest ambition...and my deepest, most fervent dream is to have a huge family. I want to be mom to a ton of kids. Does that sound crazy for a modern career woman to say? I think I would die if I could never have any more children."

In his hiding place around the corner, Josh felt stung. Punched in the gut. If he had harbored even a tick of hope for a future for him, Clair and Jimmy somewhere in his subconscious, it was now over. She wanted the one thing in the world he could never give.

He'd been blindsided by a hidden desire to keep the gorgeous woman and her son in his life for good.

An empty, fruitless desire in his empty, fruitless life.

It figured.

Chapter 6

"So you snuck your son away from your ex-husband's mansion in Abu Fujarah and managed to fly out of the country on a private jet? Wow. Cool." Maggie finished the dinner dishes and sat down at the kitchen table to join in the conversation. "But what about the U.S. Embassy? Couldn't they have helped?"

Throwing a glance over to where Jimmy played quietly on the floor, Clare leaned back in her chair and tried to get a better handle on the three Ryan siblings sitting around the table. The inner workings of Josh's mind had been frustrating her for a day and a half. She wasn't clairvoyant or a psychic, but she did have a reporter's instincts—a nose for news. And she could tell the three of them had some secret or secrets that they were withholding from the world.

Clare's intuition telegraphed a warning that each of these people was guarding a heavy load of guilt and pain behind kind eyes. It exhausted her just looking at them.

"When Ramzi first divorced me and said he would send me home without Jimmy," Clare began as she poured herself a cup of coffee from the carafe on the table, "I went to our embassy. They told me that because my baby was born an Abu Fujarah citizen, there wasn't much they could do. Apparently our treaties with that country are particularly problematic when it comes to *their* citizens. Our laws have no jurisdiction there."

Ethan had been quiet for some time, but he raised his eyes and interjected, "I understand our State Department is covertly negotiating a new oil treaty with Abu Fujarah. An end run around OPEC. I can imagine it'll be difficult for you to find anyone at State who'd be willing to help."

Maggie put a hand on her brother's arm and smiled proudly. "Ethan is a Secret Service agent, Clare. Assigned to the presidential detail. He knows people in Washington."

Clare was about to ask Ethan a question when Jimmy began to cry. He'd been happily playing with some pans and boxes on the kitchen floor, but Clare knew he was getting sleepy. She scooted her chair back, getting ready to go to him.

Josh got to his feet first. "Let me." He went to the baby, pulling him into his arms. Jimmy quieted down almost immediately, put his head on Josh's shoulder and stuck his thumb into his mouth.

"Just sit back down a minute with him if you don't mind," Clare pleaded with Josh. She felt desperate to see where this conversation might lead, desperate for any hope or any possible answer. "Let me finish my coffee, then I'll take Jimmy up and get him ready for bed."

"He's fine," Josh told her as he rejoined the group and sat down with Jimmy still in his arms. "Take your time."

Clare returned her attention to Ethan. "Can you think of anyone in Washington who might be able to give me assistance now that I've brought my son back to the U.S.?"

"Maybe. I have a buddy who works in Justice. The federal

courts are where you need to make your appeal. Our Constitution provides for children born of U.S. citizens abroad. I'll give my friend a call tomorrow, see what he thinks your chances are."

"That would be great." Clare took another sip from her mug. "I've been doing most of the yakking and y'all have been so kind to want to help me. I'd like to get to know more about you."

She smiled at Ethan. "I've heard a little about Josh's background, but it's interesting you work for the Secret Service. What's that like?"

Ethan grinned and raised his eyebrows in a wry look. "It *was* like a high-powered babysitting job, watching over top-flight politicians, diplomats and their families. *Now* it's like almost over. I gave my notice a month ago. Just three more weeks to go after I get back to work and then I'm free. Though, free for what, I'm not too sure."

Maggie jerked her coffee mug, nearly spilling the contents. "You quit? Why?"

Ethan told them the story of how the wife of a foreign diplomat he'd been guarding had come on to him, wanting to hook up. And when he'd turned her down, she'd gone to his superiors with a story about him accosting her. Lies or not, and regardless of how the investigation eventually turned out, Ethan had quickly been moved to a "nonsensitive" position. Demoted to a desk job. He had done nothing wrong but his career was ruined without recourse in a bureaucracy valuing image over truth.

"But that's just terrible," Maggie said sympathetically.

Shrugging a shoulder, Ethan smiled. "It bothered me a lot at first. I'd spent the last eight years working up to the prime detail assignments. But I'm actually getting past the worst of it now. I figure I'm just not cut out for a job where the slightest mistake or innuendo can bring you down." He gave a slight nod in Josh's direction.

There it was again. That special look passing between the siblings that said they shared dark secrets. Clare had hoped Josh's brother and sister would be able to give her a clue toward getting to the root of their brother's problems. But apparently, there wasn't much chance of any of them telling secrets anytime soon.

In fact, it seemed clear to her that the two brothers needed some time to talk alone. She turned to Josh. "I think Jimmy's already gone for the night right there in your arms. Let me have him. I'll take him up and get him settled into bed." She reached for the baby and Josh slowly released him into her arms.

"Let me help," Maggie said. "I don't get a chance to put a little one down for the night very often. It'll be fun."

Clare imagined Maggie must have seen the look passing between the brothers, too. "Okay, sure. Jimmy's pretty easy. But having company will be nice for a change."

Maggie trailed behind as Clare climbed the stairs with her beloved son in her arms. She hoped that whatever the problems the two brothers shared, they could work through them well enough to still be able to give her the help she needed to keep her baby by her side.

"So what're your plans?" Josh asked Ethan as he stood up and shook out the kinks.

"Not too sure." Ethan got up, too, and reached for the coffee pot. "I've got enough money saved up to spend the next few years on vacation."

"Would you do that? Simply not work?"

Ethan chuckled. "Brother, you are way too serious to believe. Think of all the beautiful women out there we haven't met yet. And just think of all the cool places we haven't seen, and all the hell yet to be raised.

"You're not gainfully employed at the moment," Ethan continued, turning the conversation back to Josh. "What are *your* plans?"

Josh turned his back on the little brother who had always charmed his way through life. "I'm just trying to get through one day at a time. First the funeral, then find a way to help Clare and Jimmy."

"And I suppose using Abuela's witchcraft to help those two has never occurred to you?"

Spinning around to face Ethan's grin, Josh choked out an answer. "It's occurred to me. But unlike you and Maggie, I have taken an oath not to stoop to the black arts. What if—"

"Hey, bro, hold on." Ethan held up his hand palm out to interrupt Josh's words. "You know there's nothing black about Abuela Lupe's magic. She's a white witch and a *curandera.* They use plants and the spiritual world to heal. It's the *brujas,* like great-grandmother Maria Elena Ixtepan, who are the practitioners of black magic.

"Plus, you don't see me putting any hexes on that demented woman who lied about me, do you? I don't believe in the darker creed, either."

Josh shook his head and frowned. "White, black, red. To me it's all the same. Here in the U.S. people will think you're certifiable if you practice any of it."

"Aw, come on," Ethan said with a roll of his eyes. "You've never heard of rich people getting their auras read? Or of movie stars making pilgrimages to have spiritual cleansings? White magic is cool, Josh. Don't be such a goober." Ethan leaned his butt against the counter and crossed his ankles in a relaxed pose.

Josh didn't want to talk about the family witchcraft with his brother. Ethan would never understand his desire to be normal. To not have to hide any part of who or what he was. Ethan relished being a little different. Josh knew his brother thought the magic was what separated them from their father and made them special—better. But that wasn't what Josh thought of his family's "heritage."

"Fine." Feeling irritated, Josh tried to calm down so he could talk to his brother about the important things. "Use the magic if you want. But don't mention it around Clare. I don't want her to decide we should all be put away in some freak farm.

"Help me to help her," he pleaded with his brother. "The faster we find someone to get her what she wants, the faster we can all go on with our lives."

Ethan studied him a moment. "You saying you're not interested in a more…um…involved long-term relationship with the woman?" Waiting a second for a reply that never came, Ethan's face broke into one of his wide, crazy-ass grins. "No? Well, you don't mind if I give it a shot then, do you? She's got one hell of a nice—"

Josh fisted his hands and took a step in his brother's direction, without really knowing why he suddenly felt so angry. "Just shut the hell up. Stop being an ass. She's too strong and independent to be of any real interest to someone like you."

Ethan laughed. "Oh, man. Are you ever screwed."

Upstairs, Clare stood to the side and watched as Maggie got Jimmy ready for bed. After she laid him on his side, he snuggled into the down-filled mattress and curled his knees up under his chest, seemingly dead to the world. Maggie gently placed a thin blanket over his legs and the two women backed up to the other side of the room, standing quietly in the low light, reluctant to walk away from the sight of such complete innocence.

"You're really good with babies," Clare whispered.

Maggie nodded absently as she kept her gaze trained on Jimmy.

"Do you want to have your own?" The minute the words were out of Clare's mouth, she knew how rude they sounded. But she couldn't take them back.

"There's nothing I'd like better," Maggie answered, still not taking her eyes off the baby. "But it won't happen. It can't happen. Not even if I suddenly found the right guy."

She'd been more than a little rude, Clare realized. She'd brought up a sensitive subject, and now she couldn't figure out how to back away from the topic without making things a whole lot worse.

"Um. Well, maybe one or both of your brothers will make you an aunt one of these days and—"

Maggie interrupted by turning those intense green eyes in her direction and touching her arm. "Here's the thing, Clare. This is a family problem. None of us will have children. It's not in the stars for us."

Well, that must be one downright disastrous genetic trait! A good way to end the human race. Clare chuckled to herself as she imagined Maggie must be joking. Getting even with her for being so nosy.

"Okay, I deserved that answer," Clare said. "I'm sorry I butted my nose into something that's none of my business."

"I wasn't joking," Maggie told her, clearly serious and intent. "And this is not a noble choice we're making as some other families have done so they won't pass on bad genetic traits. Our genes are fine, even if our family is not."

"I...I don't mean to pry," Clare interrupted, ready to pry anyway. "But y'all are the same Ryan family that owns the Delgado Ranch, aren't you?" She couldn't imagine how people from such a wealthy and powerful family wouldn't want to have a new generation in order to pass along that heritage.

"Yes, our father inherited the Delgado from my mother's father. But there are two sides to our family. The Irish-American Ryan side *and* our grandmother Delgado's ancient Mexican ancestry. The two don't mix well."

Clare was curious, but bit her tongue rather than say something else rude. This wasn't any of her business.

"I know Josh doesn't want me to talk about it, but I think you need to know." Maggie stared at her through the lamplight. "It's a long story, one you probably don't want to hear, filled with tragedy and rage. The bottom line is that none of the three of us can have kids. And we also won't cross into Delgado Ranch land without good reason."

This was going to be another very rude and untoward remark, but Clare had to ask. "I don't understand why not. Were you injured in an accident or something?"

"In a matter of speaking. There was an airplane accident. Fifteen years ago. We kids weren't physically in it, but our mother was killed. The circumstances brought out a lot of family anger. And in the end, the three of us got the worst of the trouble because we more or less sided with our father. We don't really take his side anymore, but it's far too late for redemption."

Maggie took a breath. "You may not believe what I have to say, but I'm about to tell you the God's truth. We're cursed. None of the Ryan family children will ever have children of their own."

"Cursed?"

"Don't laugh. I know it's hard to accept. It was hard for us at first, too. But it won't matter whether you believe me or not, because the three of us have to live knowing the truth.

"Just be a friend, will you?" Maggie pleaded. "And whatever you do, don't tell Josh I told you."

Clare could scarcely imagine that a seemingly intelligent woman like this could believe in such a fantasy. But as she looked into Maggie's eyes, the other woman's honesty shone through as clear as a Texas sky. Maggie accepted every word she'd just said as an absolute fact.

"You're sure Josh and Ethan buy into this whole curse thing, too?"

"Absolutely. You've seen how much both of them love kids. In fact, I would imagine you've already been guessing about the irony of three people who love kids as much as we do not having our own."

Yes, she had noticed. But…but… Swell. The last thing Clare needed in her life right now was an entire family, and most especially one hot cowboy Ranger, who believed in curses.

Not that it was really going to be pertinent in the long haul. As soon as she found a way to keep Jimmy with her in this country for good, Clare was going to begin a new life. Find a home, maybe go back to her old hometown of Midland. Perhaps even consider going back to work as a reporter.

That these people had a skewed view of reality and believed in curses—and heaven only knew what else—wasn't important in the big scheme of things. They were kind and seemed otherwise normal. And they were ready and able to help her in every way that mattered. She would just keep a closer eye on whatever they did or did not do that might affect Jimmy. But she wasn't truly worried. No one could be better with her baby than Maggie had been. And clearly Jimmy had formed a real attachment to Josh.

Josh. Damn.

Clare needed this family's help so desperately. But working with Josh and still walking away at the end was going to be harder than she'd thought at first.

Shoot. Her eyes welled up as she and Maggie backed out of Jimmy's room. If the Ryans really believed what Maggie said they did, then she felt terribly sorry for them. What an awful way to go through life. She'd already started to care for each of them, and she still wanted Josh's help. She still wanted Josh—period. She'd so hoped…

It just went to show that you couldn't ever trust your body or your mind to recognize a good thing. She should have learned that lesson before. But this time—this time, her heart had become involved too soon.

From here on out, Clare vowed to be far more practical. The Ryan family was her best bet for getting help, so she would not hesitate to ask for it. If she also decided she needed Josh Ryan's—um—very sexy body, then she would ask for that, too. Without letting her emotions get involved.

Hmm. Sounded good. Just like her original plan to get away from Ramzi's men here in the U.S. had at first.

Yeah? And look how well that had gone so far.

Josh sat in the rocking chair on the back porch of his Grandfather Will's house until it was nearly daylight, thinking of how best to help Clare and Jimmy. But nothing seemed clear. He was a man of gut hunches and spontaneous insights. A man who took orders and carried them out to the best of his abilities. Maggie had always been the Ryan who made the plans and liked the little details.

The more he thought about the two needy souls asleep upstairs, the two new friends looking for a regular life, the more he felt convinced that he must find some way to help them. And not just because he'd had a semi hard-on for Clare since the moment he'd met her. Though that was hard—pun intended—to miss.

No, the runaway woman and her child had touched him. Made him feel things he hadn't wanted to feel in a long, long time. Had actually thought he would never feel again.

As a kid, he'd prided himself on being able to see the big picture and reaching for the impossible. But since the day of his last firefight, the day he'd been powerless to help his combat buddy survive, he had tried to drown that ability, first in booze and then in self-pity. Had he pushed aside his dreams for so long that he'd totally lost the capability of wishing?

Thinking about such complicated matters gave him a headache. Clearly he'd been avoiding looking at both the past and the future—since that future couldn't include a family and kids of his own. And wasn't that a rip? He'd never even known family would become important to him. Never gave it a thought one way or the other. Until the day the possibility had been taken away entirely.

Hell. He might as well admit it. Dwelling on the big picture also meant he would have to give due consideration to the witchcraft and his family's heritage. But he couldn't reconcile either of those with his mental images of Clare and her child. Or maybe it was just that he didn't want to.

Whatever. He still did have one family—a brother and sister who seemed willing to help. So he would depend on them. Up to a point.

Clare stood in the last row at the cemetery, waiting until the crowd cleared out and everyone had given the Ryan grandchildren their sympathies. The funeral service had been a much bigger deal than she would have imagined for such a small rural town. People had come from all over the world to pay their respects. Cops came from San Antonio, where Will Ryan had served. Distant cousins flew in from Ireland. Clients who had used his private investigative services and had called him a friend hailed from everywhere.

Good thing she'd left Jimmy with Lara, the next-door neighbor with the day care center. Thank heaven her baby boy hadn't been at the church, disrupting the services when he became overly tired. At day care, several other kids were available for him to play with, and he'd seemed thrilled with his new playmates. Her baby hadn't appeared so happy and easygoing since—well, since forever.

Suddenly melancholy, Clare turned away from the large canopy where the family had gathered only to look up and see Josh walking toward her.

"Want to go on back?" he asked. "Are you worried about Jimmy?"

She shook her head. "Not really. I believe he's safe with Lara. And surely Ramzi's men could never locate us here in Zavala Springs. Not in a million years of looking."

"I wouldn't go quite that far." Josh put his hand on her shoulder. "Given enough time and money, anyone can be found. But for the next few days at least, we should be okay here."

Clare turned, looking up into his sunglass-covered eyes. "Your grandfather was well liked. I've talked to a couple of his clients who were also friends. They say they think Maggie can handle his business just fine, but they'll miss him terribly anyway.

"How are you holding up?" she added, gentling her voice. "Will this graveside ceremony be the last of the services for your grandfather?"

Josh flashed her a slow, sexy smile. "You heard the church eulogies. My grandfather's parents were born in Ireland. The Irish have strict rules about such things. No one leaves a funeral until they've toasted to the deceased enough for everyone to be at least three-quarters drunk. We're holding the wake at Grand-dad's house. Maggie already has it well in hand."

"Oh, yes. I'd forgotten the hours of cooking she was doing yesterday. Is it going to be like a big party?"

"Sort of. But with lots of old stories and many pleasant tears shed over several rounds of beer, telling tales about what a great guy my grandfather was.

"I've already talked to my sister and brother," Josh added. "And we've agreed to cut the gathering off early and send every-one packing before the crowd gets too out of hand. We would've pretty much done that anyway. But now we would rather spend the time tonight figuring out the best plan for helping you and Jimmy."

"Really?" Clare felt beyond touched and choked up. This family was truly special. In the best way. "I hope that won't put too much of a strain on you three. You don't need my problems on top of your own."

"No strain." Josh reached over and slowly stroked a finger down her cheek, following the path of a wayward tear. "How about a smile? Let us look out for you. It'll give us something to take our minds off other problems."

His gentle caress caused just enough zing of arousal to confuse the issue and throw her off. "Don't look out for me, Josh. I can take care of myself. Just help me worry about the baby."

Well, that sounded annoyed, and she certainly hadn't meant it that way. The nerves right under her skin had suddenly pulsed to life. The rest of her body took up the beat, tingling with his nearness.

"Uh, I've been meaning to ask about your father." She took a small step backward and changed the subject. "He's still alive, right? Your grandfather was his father. So is he here?"

Josh lifted his head and glanced around. "Right over there." Tilting his chin, he directed her gaze toward a nicely dressed man in a Stetson hat and western suit who stood apart from the others at the edge of cemetery.

As Clare studied the Ryan patriarch, who resembled Josh but looked more like a slightly shorter, heavier-set version of Ethan, the man twisted his head to look around as if he knew someone was watching. His gaze met hers. And without warning, she felt weird, as though he were studying her under a microscope. But why would he look at her that way?

Why would the wealthy, powerful owner of the Delgado Ranch care one thing about a complete stranger who didn't have anything he might need?

Clare backed up a step. Was this hugely rich oil man, Josh's father, one of Ramzi's business clients? Had she perhaps even met Mr. Ryan before in Abu Fujarah?

Oh my God. She couldn't have inadvertently stepped right into Ramzi's sphere of influence, could she? Not right here in rural Texas.

Not right here where she'd thought they would be so safe.

Chapter 7

"Another cup of coffee?" Josh noticed his hand shaking, the one holding the hours-old pot of coffee, and changed his mind about needing any more caffeine. "Anyone interested before I pitch the rest of this?"

He'd managed to make it through an entire Irish wake without so much as one sip of booze. Nice work, but it didn't mean his problems were over. Now that they'd been working on Clare's plan for several hours and almost had it worked out, he admitted his shaky hands were coming from far more than just too much coffee.

Were the shrinks right about him having PTSD? Or could it be pure panic about taking on the responsibility for Clare's life that was making his hands shake?

Three sets of tired eyes met his, and three heads shook in unison. The four of them had been at this for what seemed like forever, since the end of the wake. Jimmy had been put to bed hours ago.

"None for me. I think we're nearly done with the details,"

Maggie said absently. Bending her head to the yellow pad on the kitchen table, she slipped the pencil into her mouth, rereading and considering what she'd already written. "I think we need a backup plan. Maybe more than one. But it would take some research and we don't have the time."

Josh slid a glance in Clare's direction and noticed how exhausted she looked as she leaned her elbows on the table. He wanted to give her comfort, take some of the worry from her shoulders. But he'd already done everything he could think of—except taking her in his arms. And although that's what his body ached to do, he wasn't getting that close to her. Any closer than a few feet would lead to things decidedly pleasurable but also decidedly risky. He didn't imagine Clare would accept anything physical between them anyway.

But the more he looked at her across the table, the more he liked what he saw—and hungered to taste. Her sensual appeal shone through the tiny worry lines and purple smudges under her eyes. Her slender body and delicate features spoke to him in ways he could only dream of.

Holding her. Kissing her senseless. Touching her in the all places he'd fantasized about. Doing things that might at first soothe, but in the end would stir sensations that were raw and electrifying. None of it was in the stars for them.

But he couldn't push the rampant sensual visions out of his mind. He was far too aware of her for either of their sakes.

He fought to bend his mind away from its current direction. His thoughts turned to Clare's competent mothering skills and her loving ways with Jimmy. He couldn't seem to shake free of the images of a sensual Clare and all her wonders. He admired the way she battled unseen forces for her son. She characterized everything he'd ever respected in a woman. And he couldn't let himself respond to any of it.

"Even though my brain is fried tonight," Maggie began as

she made one final checkmark on her legal pad, "I think we've come up with the best plan possible. Well…considering the limitations.

"But it all depends on you, Clare," she added. "What are your thoughts?"

"I don't see that I have a lot of choices," Clare said with a weary sigh. "But if you're asking if I can stand to leave Jimmy with you and Lara while I go off to Washington to find help at the Justice Department, the answer is yes. I know he'll be temporarily safer here than with me.

"Or if you're asking if I care about this plan being not totally legal, the answer is no. But…" Her voice trailed off with a crack of tension.

Josh moved beside her and laid his hand over hers on the table. "What's bothering you? I happen to believe you have terrific instincts. You wouldn't have made it this far without them. If you're worried about any part of the plan, then let us work something else out."

"It's not the plan, it's… It's y'all's father. When I saw him today at the cemetery he seemed to recognize me. Or at least he was studying me closely for some reason. He's an oil man. What if he's friends with Ramzi? What if he tells my ex he saw me here?"

Ethan was on his feet in an instant. "Brody Ryan had better not open his big loud mouth about seeing you. Not to his powerful oil baron buddies. Not to anyone."

Maggie reached up and took Ethan's hand. "We don't know that he will, brother. He might not have even recognized her. Don't go painting the man any blacker than he already is.

"Jumping to conclusions isn't going to get us anywhere," Maggie continued. "What we need is a—"

"Plan." They all spoke the word together, and then chuckled as Maggie looked flustered.

"Right," she said as the sudden red flush faded from her

cheeks. "One of us is going to have to question our father about his odd reaction to seeing Clare. It can't be Ethan, though."

"Why the hell not?" Ethan sputtered.

"Because every time someone even mentions his name you flare into a rage. That wouldn't make for a good, subjective interview."

"Interview?" Ethan groaned under his breath. "You're starting to talk like Grandpa Will, Mags. We don't need to interview our own father. He'll just damn well tell us what we want to know."

"If I sound like a P.I. it's because that's what I am," Maggie said with a sniff. "I've been partnering with Granddad for the last few years. He left me the business and I intend to keep running it if I can find a way to make it pay."

Maggie turned to Josh.

"I'll do it," Josh heard himself say. "First thing tomorrow. He won't lie to me."

"Dad may be a lot of things, Josh," Maggie said. "But he's never been a liar. Just ask him straight out. He'll tell you.

"While you're at the Delgado," Maggie went on, "Ethan, Clare and I will work out a few of the other details we've talked about for our plan."

Josh turned to Ethan. "When I get back, you and I can go over the bodyguarding details before Clare and I head out to catch our plane."

Ethan nodded. "I'll round up someone to get that weapon you wanted and have it waiting for you in D.C. And…I'll be watching out for these two independent females when they visit Maggie's old friend."

Both Maggie and Clare sat up with their backs ramrod straight and their lips turned down in frowns. "We don't need a babysitter," Maggie said indignantly.

Ethan forced a grin as he muttered, "Yeah, I guess you're both big, bad tough guys, all right. But guarding is what I do. Let me help the best way I know how, will you?"

"Yeah," Josh piped in. "Just take whatever help is offered."

Feeling relieved that Ethan would be accompanying Clare and Maggie on their errand, Josh checked Clare's face for any sign she would try to get out of Ethan's assistance. Watching Clare's back during every minute of this operation was imperative for its success. And also for his peace of mind. He just wished someone would be watching his back, too. There couldn't be any chance of him screwing up like he'd done on his last mission. There simply *could not* be any mistakes. This time it would kill him for sure.

"That's enough. I need sleep," Maggie said as she rose from the table. "We should all get at least a few hours. Tomorrow will be a long day."

Josh caught himself drooling at the sight of Clare standing and stretching her back. Tomorrow, hell. *Tonight* was going to be one of the longest nights of his life.

There wouldn't be much sleep for him knowing she was right upstairs alone in the big bed that had belonged to his grandparents. Shaking out his pant legs and turning his back, Josh chastised himself again. Stupid ass. It was past time to get those sorts of erotic pictures out of his mind for good. He needed all of his senses to keep Clare safe. So he would not be thinking of her like that again.

Of course he wouldn't. He was going to stop just as soon as horses flew and sheep turned into fighting Marines. Roger that.

Clare wondered if she had any brains left at all, or if living under the same roof with Josh had left her mindless as well as boneless from the constant sexual tension. The man distracted her, cost her focus and determination when focus and determination were the very things she needed the most. Damn him. She could not afford this kind of nonsense.

Even here, riding in Maggie's SUV, she still couldn't get him out of her mind and he was probably thirty miles away. That made him infuriatingly dangerous.

The hot sun beat down on the roof of the vehicle as early morning gave way to midday. Butterflies and honeybees flitted through hazy sunlight and multicolored wildflowers lined the roadways outside her passenger window. Brilliant orange indian paintbrush, spectacular yellow black-eyed Susans and the splashy azure blue sage. Beautiful at this time of year, but not enough to make her stop wondering how Josh was getting along on his errand to the Delgado. She knew he couldn't think straight when it came to his father, and she hoped he could manage not to get into an argument—or worse.

Turning her head, she glanced at Ethan, who was sitting at attention in the backseat. Maggie drove the three of them along the rural caliche road, heading toward their destination. And none of them had said much for several miles.

Running this particular errand made Clare nervous. It must have made Ethan nervous, as well, because before they'd left the house he'd hauled pieces of a handgun out of his luggage. He'd fit the pieces together and then loaded it before holstering the scary thing under the waistband of his jeans.

That had made Clare more nervous than ever.

What the heck was she doing? At the very least she'd been intelligent enough to leave Jimmy behind at the day care center again today. But maybe she should have stayed back there, too.

"Is this going to be dangerous?" she asked Maggie.

Maggie screwed up her mouth as she navigated a small dip in the road. "Not at all. I called Hector this morning and told him we were on our way out. I've known him almost my whole life. He used to make up phony IDs for us as teenagers when we wanted to go dancing at one of the honky-tonks but weren't old enough. And then for a while he sold immigration papers to

Mexicans who'd already come across the border but needed ID in order to work. He did a little time in the federal pen for that one, so he doesn't make up IDs at all anymore. He only agreed to do this one because he owes me a favor.

"All you have to do is smile pretty for the camera, pay the man his hundred bucks and we're outta there."

"And this is definitely illegal, right?" Clare knew the answer, but wished she didn't.

"Definitely." Ethan had been quiet in the backseat, but he chimed in to answer just as Maggie drove over a rise and a one-story ranch house came into view.

Both Josh and Ethan had disapproved of this one part of their plan. She wasn't crazy about paying a known criminal in order to obtain a phony ID, either, but she'd decided she would do almost anything if it led to a way of keeping Jimmy.

The man Maggie called Hector greeted them outside the house. *"Buenos dias, Margarita y compadres,"* he said before he grabbed Maggie up in a great bear hug.

Ethan relaxed when the man shook his hand. And Clare finally took the first real breath she'd had in hours.

Twenty minutes after arriving at Hector's house, they were back in the SUV headed toward town. And she was in the not-so-proud possession of a driver's license that listed her name as Clare Ryan of Zavala Springs, Texas.

Getting the phony ID made up hadn't been scary at all. But the idea of flying to Washington, D.C., on a commercial airline posing as Josh's wife was making her knees knock and her mouth go dry.

Ramzi wouldn't be able to figure their plan out. It wouldn't be possible. The man couldn't read minds. And his men weren't on the lookout for a man and wife traveling together without a baby. So she wasn't too worried about him. But posing as Josh's wife meant the two of them would be staying close. And it would also mean at least one night with just the two of them in a motel room.

Could she do it? Could she keep him at arm's length and simply do the things that she must in order to begin her new future with her son? Having Jimmy around had kept her from acting on her impulses so far. But without her baby between them, what would happen? This crazy sexual draw she'd felt for Josh was beyond her experience. Could she take control of it and act like the civilized and determined woman she was?

The guy drove her nuts. She had to keep reminding herself that he loved kids but had convinced himself he would never have any. He must remain completely off her radar and off-limits.

Instead, fool that she was, she kept dreaming of ways to push him right past both of their limits.

Josh had known the moment his father's hands spotted him on Delgado land. So it was no surprise when both he and the old man pulled up their trucks into the ranch house's wide drive at the exact same time.

Good. If they were outside together, maybe Josh could ask his questions on the veranda and save himself from having to set foot inside the house that would no doubt remind him too much of the mother he'd loved and lost so many years ago. A leaden lump formed in his throat.

Man, Josh wished he hadn't been the best person to interview Brody Ryan about Clare. Thoughts of his beloved mother had been stuffed away behind all the other family problems for a good long while. But coming here, seeing the house she'd built together with her husband when their three kids had been babies and she'd been so in love…once again being in the place where he'd been raised… It all brought up stinging, heartrending memories and left him antsy and shaken.

"Wanna come on in?" Brody asked him. "Conchita will make us cold drinks, or something to eat if you'd rather."

Josh shook his head and stuck his hands in his pockets.

"Nothing, thanks. Let's just sit outside. I won't take up much of your time."

After they were seated around a wrought iron table under the shade of a cottonwood tree, Brody leaned back in his chair and studied Josh. "You doing okay now, son? The funeral wasn't too hard on you yesterday, was it?"

"What makes you think I wouldn't be just fine?" Josh's temper immediately flared. "Why not ask how Maggie or Ethan handled the service instead of me?"

Brody raised his hands in surrender. "It's my understanding you're the one who's recently licked an alcohol problem, son. Funerals can be mighty stressful. And I know how much you loved your grandfather."

"Yeah? What do you know about love? You never even loved your own father. You used to say he was a foolish old man for wanting to be a cop and a P.I. You—"

Brody shook his head sadly and interrupted. "There's a world of difference between respect and love, boy. When I was your age, I thought my father was being irresponsible for wanting to be a cop instead of coming into ranching with me. There was a good life waiting for him and Mom on the Delgado, I would have seen to it. But your grandfather insisted he still had duties to fulfill. He was all tied up in some noble idea of law and order. Some ridiculous notion of generations of Ryans working for the little guy.

"But I never stopped loving him," Brody added quietly. "Why else would I have agreed to let him take in my baby girl when her mama died?"

"Agreed?" Josh's blood pressure shot through the roof as he balled his fists. "You couldn't wait to get all of us out of your hair. Me to the army, Ethan to college and Maggie with Grandpa and Nana. You wanted us gone, so we went. Don't act so damned surprised now that none of us want to come back home."

Brody narrowed his lips and stared out over the corrals toward the foaling barns. After a moment he said, "None of you tried to understand me. I mean, I knew Maggie was too young to know, but I thought you would've…" His voice trailed off as he slowly shook his head.

"I had my own guilt and grief to work through back then." Brody's low voice came out in rasps, with mournful sighs and resounding sorrow. "Didn't it ever occur to you that my children reminded me so much of their mama I couldn't breathe just looking at them? I missed her so badly I wanted to cry and rage at the world. I couldn't have you three around to see your daddy like that. I just needed time and a little space. I didn't want it to be forever."

Stunned speechless, Josh took a deep breath. Thousands of questions rolled through his mind, but he wouldn't ask. Despite what Maggie had said, their father was a notorious liar. All his business acquaintances knew that Brody Ryan looked out for number one, no matter what he had to do or say to get there. Josh didn't for a minute believe what his old man had just said. Love had never been in Brody's vocabulary. And why would that have changed?

But let him try to lie when Josh questioned him about Clare. Let him try.

"Did you notice the woman who came to the funeral services with us yesterday?" Josh spit the question out quickly, going for the element of surprise.

Brody took no more than an instant to shake off his sudden start at Josh's change of topic. "The young pretty one? She would've been hard to miss."

"Had you met her before? Did you recognize her?"

"In a way, I did recognize her."

Josh's heart skipped a beat. See there? His father didn't dare lie to him. Josh would've seen a lie for what it was and called him on it. But now what was he going to do about the truth?

Just in case, Josh decided to be an adult for once and feel out the situation a little more before he jumped in and took a swing. "Where did you meet her?"

"I've never laid eyes on the girl before yesterday."

"But then how did you recognize her?" Had Clare's picture been printed next to one of her *Oil News* bylines?

Brody actually smiled, but in a sad, melancholy way. "It wasn't exactly the girl that I knew, Josh. It was more the looks bouncing between the two of you that I recognized. It's been a long time since I'd had the pleasure of seeing one of those loving looks in your mama's eyes whenever she glanced my way. But I still couldn't miss one of those love-filled gazes when I saw one."

"But you're wrong," Josh insisted as forcefully as he could without jumping down his old man's throat. "We don't love each other. We're not even dating. She's almost a stranger. You couldn't have seen—"

"You can try lying to yourself, son. But I see the truth written on your face right here, and I'm calling you on it."

That did it. Josh stood, clenching his jaw and freeing his hands, prepared to knock that lying smile right off his father's face.

Brody stood to face him down. "Easy, there. I'm glad you've found someone. She looks like a strong-willed and determined young woman with a good head. Reminds me of your mama. If anyone can help you settle down, she'd be the one.

"I want to meet her," Brody continued soothingly. "Why don't you bring her here to the Delgado for supper? Anytime. Just say the word."

For the second time in as many days, Josh's temper got the best of him around his father. But he couldn't bring himself to really strike the man. It would've made his mother sad.

Without a word, he stormed away from the father who had always made his blood boil and his mind go blank. The father who had never before spoken a word about love. The father he had hated for nearly half of his life.

And Maggie thought Ethan flared up at the mention of Brody's name? Hah!

As of this moment he didn't care if he ever saw his father again. He couldn't get his feelings in line whenever they were together.

So Josh walked quickly back to his truck. Before any of the words his father had spoken could make him change his mind and do something crazy—like knock the old man to the ground— or stay and listen to his lies.

Chapter 8

"Ya got that?" Ethan asked.

It was much later that afternoon and Josh had just listened to a ten-minute dissertation on bodyguard practices and had spent another five minutes reviewing plans on how to reach the meeting place in D.C. where the Justice Department official would be waiting. He'd thought his temper was under control, but found out it simmered right under the surface.

"Geez, bubba," Josh said. "Didn't know this stuff could be so complicated. Maybe you should play my part and act as Clare's husband, delivering her safely to D.C."

Ethan raised his eyebrows, but the twinkle in his eyes gave Josh a hint of what was coming. "I'd need to request more of a leave, but if you're sure you want *me* accompanying Clare, then sure. That's my idea of a dream detail."

Ethan's silly grin should've taken the real sting out of the ribbing, but it didn't. Josh only felt an increasing desperation to get this job over with. To rid himself of this awful enchantment, the spell he'd apparently fallen under where this woman and her child were concerned. To put an end to his growing temptation to follow through on what would no doubt be his biggest mistake ever. As it was, Clare's face would bother his dreams for the rest of his life. And her body, built to nurture a man's spiritual as well as physical needs, would haunt him endlessly.

The two of them would be together for only a few more days at most. After all, she was merely using him to get what she needed and then would be on her way.

The using him part didn't bother him too much. He was on the same wavelength with her about fighting to keep her and her son together. Wanted it badly enough, in fact, that he'd do anything she needed. The idea of her son going off to some faraway land forever without his mother made Josh resolve to find a permanent solution and an end to this quest, no matter what.

The fact that she would be leaving after things had finally been settled on Jimmy's status could only be for the best. He understood that he was not the man of her dreams. The one who would give her a whole house full of babies and a normal world. Whether they slept together or not, she would be moving on with her life in the end.

So, as much as he wanted her, bedding Clare Chandler and watching her go would be too much like him using her for a temporary feel-good time. Like a payment for his services. It would damn him to hell for eternity.

Try telling that to his ever-ready body.

Even in his inevitable rock-hard and tense mode, he swore he wouldn't throw caution to the wind and haul her into his arms. Not when he'd realized something about himself in the last few hours. If he made love with Clare, it would be just that for him— love. His father, as much as he hated to admit it, had been right. At least from his side of it. She meant something huge in his life, and if he slept with her, there would be no going back.

"All right," Ethan said, breaking into Josh's wayward thoughts. "One last lesson. You want both the airport and the motel experience to go smoothly. Those places are where your greatest chance of Clare being accosted will come.

"Remain aware at all times. Watch people's eyes and facial expressions as they get near Clare. Watch their body movements. Learn to scan everything and everyone quickly so you'll have enough time to react. Her ex-husband could've hired any kind of muscle, so everyone you meet has the potential to do her harm. This detail, the whole reason you're along, is solely for her protection. Got that?"

Oh, Josh got it, all right. This would not turn out like his last firefight. He would protect her or die.

But then, who the hell was going to protect him from himself?

"Stop at that discount store up ahead," Clare told Josh in a tone that she hoped meant no quibbling.

She and Josh, without Jimmy, were an hour and a half from Zavala Springs on their way to the San Antonio airport in Lucille, and she was getting more uptight and irritable with every mile. It wasn't like her. But not having Jimmy sitting beside made her feel as if someone had taken her right arm. She'd already experienced one massive attack of guilt and unease at leaving him behind—but something else was bothering her, too. Josh had shaved for their trip, and the masculine scent of his aftershave reminded her that the reality of the two them being alone together was a force to contend with. Sadly, she figured that to be a losing battle.

"We don't have a lot of extra time before we have to catch the plane," Josh said without taking his eyes from the road ahead. "Don't forget the schedule."

"If we have any chance at all of making this act work at the airport or anywhere else, then we need to buy you some new clothes and something more…uh…suburban in the way of luggage."

"What? What's wrong with what I've got?"

She tried to hide her smile. "Well, I personally like the big, bad Ranger-slash-cowboy look on you. It's…sexy. But I don't think it goes along well with the idea of a man bringing his wife with him to D.C. on business. Do you?"

"Sexy?" Josh darted her a dark look. "What do you suggest instead?"

"Maggie and I stopped at that discount store earlier today when we bought the cell phone for you to carry. I got myself this nice plain pantsuit and a small carry-on. I'm sure we can find something for you that's a little less edgy than what you have."

Josh's jaw tightened but he calmly turned into the parking lot. "Less edgy, huh? I can hardly wait."

A few moments later, Josh reluctantly climbed out of the truck, jammed the Stetson lower on his forehead and followed a sprightly Clare as she marched through the automatic sliding doors. She headed straight to the men's clothes and began checking out the racks of pants. The first pair she put her hand on were navy polyester and Josh's stomach turned.

"What size do you wear?" she asked without turning from the rack.

God save him. The woman had gotten him all tangled up, and he could barely utter a sound. It would be one thing for them to playact as husband and wife on an airplane, but to have her choosing his clothes felt much too intimate.

He stood silently swearing at himself for his own foolishness at ever agreeing to this crazy plan in the first place. But the more he watched her diligently searching the racks, the more he found himself captivated by the curve of her shoulder and the way her hair curled down her neck.

And so, in spite of his efforts not to, Josh lost control of the situation.

She turned to stare at him, while her fingers tapped lightly on the hanger in her hand. "Earth to Josh. I thought we'd agreed you need to look like someone who's going to a business meeting. Quit staring at me. Just which one of us will make us late now?"

Lord have mercy. "There's only one way any kind of businessman coming from Texas would dress," he muttered. "Leave it to me. You go round up whatever luggage you think looks better than my duffel."

Clare bristled but shut her mouth and went to look at the luggage. She wondered if this whole idea had been smart after all. Josh had been touchy ever since he'd gone to see his father. So touchy, yet so damned sexy she could barely concentrate. Swallowing down the wave of lust she felt every time he was nearby, she decided that for right now, she would act instead of think.

Not long afterward, she rolled a superlight, upright carry-on bag in a tasteful shade of dark gray toward the checkout cashiers at the front of the store. From the corner of her eye she saw Josh with his back to her as he stood peering into a glass-fronted counter. He was wearing a pair of dress jeans and a long-sleeved dress shirt in a muted denim shade of blue. And when he turned, she saw he had on an impressive red-striped tie. Clare was touched by his quick change and nearly dumbfounded with the picture he made of the clean-cut Texas businessman.

She made a U-turn in the middle of the aisle and walked up beside him just as his gaze seemed to be searching the store aisles.

"There you are, darlin'," he said when he spotted her. He reached out and drew her close. "I want your opinion on something."

It pleased her to think he'd been looking for her. Maybe it pleased her a little bit too much. She didn't want him to keep getting to her like this. Their situation was difficult enough.

When she got close enough to see, she discovered the glass case was the jewelry counter. Then she noticed the expression on the face of the woman behind it, and Clare was floored. The woman was giving her a "you got it made, girl" kind of look. A look that clearly said the middle-aged woman wished she'd hooked a man like Josh.

Josh picked up a braided silver band and held it out to her. "This ring isn't that fancy, but it made me somehow think of you. You can't be married without rings, you know." He winked at her as if to let her know this was all just part of the act.

But Clare didn't feel like acting. Torn between pulse-spiking desire and total disbelief, she could only give him a weak smile.

His grin faltered as she silently stood there staring down at the ring in his hand as if it were a bomb. "You don't like it. My fault. But I was just trying to do the right thing. If you would rather have one of those platinum and diamond rings, that'll be fine."

"N-n-no," she sputtered, feeling as though her insides were sliding into a pool of warm chocolate. "I wouldn't trade it for... Um. I mean, nothing wrong with this one."

Her knees knocked together as she tried the plain band on her ring finger. It fit perfectly. In fact, the way the ring fit and looked after she'd put it on her finger quickly turned in her mind to a fairy tale. The story of a solid man who had picked it out, and of how much he truly loved the woman who would wear his promise on her hand for life.

If only that story wasn't just all lies in their case.

"Fits just right," she said weakly. "We'll take it."

Fifteen minutes later, they were through the checkout line and back beside Lucille. Clare's head was spinning. She couldn't stop sneaking peeks at her left hand. Cripes. She'd been the one who'd started this whole impossible journey, but now things were moving beyond her control.

Josh tore the tags off the new piece of luggage and crammed

a few of his things inside, then turned to her. Sunlight gleamed in his rich dark-brown hair. His coffee-colored eyes darkened to ebony and filled with something she would swear seemed like passion.

He touched her cheek. "You were right. About the clothes and the bag. They make us look right together. A better picture for our act."

"And thank you for the rings." Only rudimentarily aware of the change in her breathing, Clare let hormones rule, stood on tiptoes and touched her lips to his with a featherlight kiss of gratitude.

But when he gasped, she let herself fall into the fantasy and deepened the kiss. Josh didn't take long to respond in kind. With lightning speed, he dug his hands into her hair and hauled her closer, wedging her body between his thighs. He cruised his mouth over hers, promising heaven with his touch and driving her wild with the primal thrust of his tongue.

The thrumming pulse ran from him to her, causing one hell of an incredibly female earthquake to course through her body. Catching her chin with gentle fingers and holding her fast, he crushed his mouth to hers, sensually exploring and tasting until the tiny quakes growing inside her turned to huge, 9.0-on-the-Richter-scale tremors.

"Josh?"

Through the haze in his head, Josh heard her say his name. It slipped off her tongue easily. Like something she said all the time without giving it a second thought. As though she'd spoken his name in hundreds of moments of companionable reflection—or in the heat of passion.

His pulse picked up speed as she clung to him. Rubbing his hands up and down her rib cage and lightly rolling his thumbs up under her breasts, he discovered something wonderful. The tiny mewling sounds she made as he stroked her body were turning him hot, hard and wild. Lost and becoming more and more impatient to be rid of the layers of clothes separating his fingers from her warmth, Josh nearly quit thinking altogether.

But while whatever was left of his brain focused on Clare, a car came up the parking-lot aisle toward them, revving its engine. Josh heard the sound in the back of his mind and actually processed what it meant. Managing to find a shred of survival instinct still intact, he dropped his hands and set her back just as the car rumbled past.

Frustration shimmied along every nerve ending. He exhaled hard, and fought to bring down the fire.

"What just happened?" Clare asked as she swayed on her feet, clearly dazed.

The bruised look of her swollen lips and the slightly mussed look of her long blond hair shocked him and nearly knocked him flat. He should've kept his damn hands off her.

"You kissed me." Josh heard the annoyance in his voice and managed to pull himself into the moment by letting that irritation have its way. "Why'd you do it?"

"I…" She looked up into his face and the prettiest shade of blush colored her cheeks. "It's not my fault. You turn my head around with your darlins' and your winks and your rings…and with your whole damn act."

"Aren't we supposed to be acting?" he asked wickedly. "I thought that's what this was all about."

She bristled, then apparently found her backbone and straightened up. "You're too good at acting. I lose track. From now on, don't improvise. Just follow your sister's plan. Okay?"

Without answering, he gritted his teeth, sucked in a breath and hustled her into the pickup. They were late enough already.

Josh watched Clare step out ahead of him, bouncing down the concourse and dragging her carry-on behind her. The play of her upper thigh muscles as she moved, clearly noticeable under the tasteful black slacks, caused a rising bulge in his jeans that he simply couldn't afford. Lordy mercy, she was something else, this "wife" of his.

Scanning the concourse, Josh checked out everyone nearby and paid attention to watching her back. It would do her no good if he watched her body movements rather than the people who could do her harm.

He could not afford to be careless. There was too much at stake.

They approached the security lineup and Josh's nerves jumped inside his skin. How would she handle it?

He narrowed the gap between them, bending to whisper in her ear. "Easy, darlin'. No sweat here. Just keep moving fast, as though your plane is about to leave without you."

Clare nodded, bent to take off her shoes and then picked up the pace. She smiled at the security guard who asked to see her ticket and ID and handed them over.

As the man studied her ID, Josh was close enough to feel the tension in her body like a living, breathing entity. "Good work on managing to get your name change handled before this trip, sugar," he said in a voice loud enough for the guard to hear. "I'm proud of you."

The guard looked over Clare's shoulder and pinned Josh with a hard stare.

Josh chuckled and raised his eyebrows like a man at his wit's end. "Newlyweds. Not always on top of things like we should be. We've got other stuff on our minds."

The security guard's lips creaked up at the sides in a ghost of a smile and he handed Clare's ticket and ID back without giving her another look. The two of them bustled their way through the X-ray machines and made it to the plane with little time to spare.

Clare buckled herself into a seat by the window and Josh sat next to her. She closed her eyes, looking tired and relieved.

He touched her arm. "Good idea. Take a nap if you can. I'll be watching out, but I don't think we have anything to worry about from here on out. That was the hardest part of the whole trip."

But he wasn't so sure. Her ex-husband was intelligent and powerful and determined to get his son back. Until they had the power of the U.S. government behind Clare, he wouldn't really consider them safe at all.

Several hours later Clare opened the motel room door, hauled her bag inside and kicked off her shoes. They'd made it. All the way to Washington, D.C.—or at the least, right outside Baltimore. Maybe this trip, this quest for the grand prize, was going to work out after all.

Josh came through the door behind her and flipped on a couple more lights. "Not much to look at, is it?" He threw his bag onto the shelf meant to hold one and looked around again. "I'm going back out to make sure no one is asking after us. I won't be gone long."

Clare widened her eyes. "Someone was following us?"

Josh grinned and stayed put. "Nah. I'm just being extra careful to backtrack our steps. Easy. We're okay."

She stood blinking first at him and then at the one big king-size bed. Feeling stuck to the spot, she suddenly wasn't all that sure she could stand being in the same room with the man. His presence overpowered the place and made the already tiny room seem smaller than it was.

What had ever possessed her to believe she could spend the entire night in the same room with a man who made her toes tingle just looking at him? Now what would she do? Sleep in the bathroom?

Every time he smiled at her, her knees wobbled. From the very first time she'd seen him, she'd been drowning in his gaze. Sinking in his laughter. Leaning on his strong shoulders when her own two feet should have been strong enough to hold her up.

Josh studied her in the soft lighting. "You okay?"

She nodded but kept silent, trying hard not to jump the man where he stood.

"You're probably just a little jet-lagged. And maybe hungry. How about while I'm out, I grab us something to eat? It shouldn't take me much time."

"Uh…okay." Anything to get him out of there so she could get her mind and body back under control.

He stared at her for a second. "Why don't you keep the cell phone and call Maggie while I'm gone? There's no way your ex could put a trace on this throwaway phone. Tell my sister we've arrived safely. And just maybe Jimmy won't be in bed yet and you'll be able to talk to him."

Clare heaved a deep sigh, letting out air she hadn't known she'd been holding inside. What a terrific man Josh Ryan had turned out to be. So thoughtful and so different from her ex-husband. Why was it that great guys always had some tremendous handicaps? It was just the way her life went, she supposed. The good guys couldn't be had, while the bad guys kept showing up and making her life miserable.

She thanked him and Josh took off, leaving the room with a big empty feeling that gaped and yawned right through her. What was she going to do about him?

After she spoke to both Maggie and Jimmy and satisfied herself that everything was fine and going according to plan, she sat for a second, staring at the phone. Both Josh and Ethan had said to never try getting in contact with anyone from her past. Not until Jimmy's status was settled. But she needed to talk to her father. Badly.

He must be frantic not hearing from her in so long. She studied the phone again. Josh had said no one could trace this cell phone. Then what would it hurt if she made a quick call to her dad?

She pushed the numbers to his cell, hoping she would reach

him no matter where in the world he was at the moment. When he answered, her legs failed her entirely and she had to sit down.

"Hi, Dad. It's me, and both Jimmy and I are safe." She rushed the words so the tears building in her eyes couldn't be heard in her voice.

"Clare! Thank God you two are okay. Where are you?"

"I can't tell you exactly. But we're in the U.S. and we've got a plan. I'm hoping by tomorrow things will be more settled. I just wanted to let you know we're okay."

"Ramzi called me." The hesitation was clear in his voice. "Looking for Jimmy. He's not happy about your leaving Abu Fujarah with his son."

"I know, Dad. But I couldn't leave without my baby."

"No, of course not. Do you need my help, Clare?"

His worried tone got to her. He was no longer a young man and she didn't want to cause him this much stress. What would it hurt to give him a little hope?

"No thanks. Tomorrow we're going to meet a friend of a friend from the Justice Department to talk about what steps I need to take. I was afraid to meet him at his office, so I made arrangements for lunch at the place you and I went in the university area, remember?"

"I remember. So this man will be able to help you keep Jimmy with you?"

"I hope so."

There was a slight lull in the conversation. She knew her father would be going through hell until he could be assured she and his grandson were safe, and she didn't want that to be his last thought before they hung up. So she asked the first question that popped into her mind.

"Daddy, how do you know when you're really in love?"

"Are you having second thoughts about divorcing Ramzi?"

"Heavens, no. I...um...was just wondering. I don't believe

I was ever truly in love with Ramzi. Just infatuated by his looks and power.

"But you and Mom were really in love once, weren't you?" Clare brought to mind a mental picture of her mother on the last day she'd ever seen her, as she was packing her bags to leave when Clare was ten years old. Hell. What was wrong with her that she would bring up the damned woman's name to the very man she'd walked away from?

"Oh, never mind," she said quickly.

But her father was answering her question anyway. "The man and woman kind of love is a crock, Clare. It's not for real. But the kind of love you have for your children, now that's forever. Keep remembering that."

"But Mom must not have loved *me* very much. Otherwise why would she have left me?" Clare could hardly believe she'd said such things to her father. She must really be losing her mind.

Her father remained silent for a tense second or two, then he finally spoke in a low tone. "Your mother didn't leave you, Clare. It was me she didn't want. Me she'd needed to be free of."

Clare was horrified at her own behavior. Over twenty years and she had never mentioned any of this to her father before now. Maybe she truly was going a little insane without Jimmy—or over her feelings for Josh.

However, despite what her father had said, Clare knew her mother hadn't really loved her at all. After the woman who'd given her life left, Clare had received a Christmas present or two and a birthday card from time to time, but she had never seen her mother's smiling face again. Had never had another hug from her, nor even so much as heard her soft voice. Such emptiness was not love as far as Clare was concerned.

"It's okay, Daddy. I do love Jimmy more than anything, and believe me, I will never walk away from him. Don't worry. We'll find a way to make this all right."

Lord how she hoped and prayed that what she'd just said would turn out to be true. Her son was the most important thing in the world to her.

She didn't like the idea of using anyone, but she had a feeling Josh and his family could make miracles happen. He would find some way of keeping them together. Of saving her son. And so, she would keep Josh close, and do whatever it took. Regardless of the consequences.

Chapter 9

Ramzi al-Hamzah looked up from his computer screen when he heard the knock at his office door. "Yes?"

"Excuse me, Excellency." The Abu Fujarah investigator, hired to locate Ramzi's son, entered the temporary office space fashioned from a spare room in his hotel suite.

"What have you heard of my son?" Ramzi's tone was harsh and impatient. The longer it took to be reunited with his boy, the more frustrated and angry he became.

"Nothing yet, sir. But you were right about the woman contacting her father. We just intercepted a cell-phone conversation between them."

"So then we know where my ex-wife is at the moment." Not a question. Ramzi expected his underlings to do the jobs they'd been hired to do.

"No. But we know the area where she will be tomorrow at

noon." The hired investigator explained that they'd listened in on her father's cell-phone conversation.

"But she didn't mention that my son was with her?" The pain of not being able to rescue his son turned to cold fury in Ramzi's heart. "Where. Is. My. Child?"

"Unknown. But we will be looking for her tomorrow. If she has the boy, you will soon have your son back."

The frustration was making Ramzi nuts. He wanted his baby back inside his own country where he belonged. That an American woman would dare to deprive him of his own flesh went beyond his imaginings.

"And what if she doesn't have my child with her? Then what?"

The man standing in front of his desk looked uncomfortable. "Perhaps we can *suggest* that she tell us where the boy is, Excellency."

"Force her?" Ramzi shook his head. "You don't know my ex-wife. She's stubborn. Reckless. Believes she has right on her side. She would die rather than sacrifice her will.

"No," Ramzi added demandingly. "Just bring her here to me if my son is not accompanying his mother."

"What if she has someone else with her? Or what if she gives us the slip? What do you want us to do then?"

The frustration of losing his boy was beginning to get the better of Ramzi. But Clare would not win this one. If it was to be a battle of wills, he knew he would win. He had been schooled in the art of getting whatever he desired by the master. His father.

Trying to calm his growing nerves about what his ex-wife's treachery might mean for the future, Ramzi answered, "Do what you must, but either bring her or my child here alive."

The man hesitated, cleared his throat and then dared to speak his thoughts aloud. "I have a contingency plan in case your son is not accompanying the mother, sir. May I tell you my humble thoughts?"

Ramzi was willing to listen to any plan that would have his

son returned. But it must be soon, at the very least before his own father showed up in this country and got involved.

He could think of no worse circumstance than having to admit defeat to the sheikh. Quite simply, that would never be allowed.

"Want the last slice of pizza?" Josh kicked off his boots and loosened his tie.

The tiny table in this equally tiny motel room was barely big enough to hold the extra-large pepperoni pizza, two longnecks and the two of them.

It had already been one tough day of trying to ignore his body's reaction to Clare, and he figured the worst might be yet to come. When he'd returned with their supper, Clare had already taken a shower and changed into her night clothes. And while the little boyish-looking shorts and the loose-fitting T-shirt she wore weren't see-through or particularly sexy, he couldn't stop gazing surreptitiously at her long legs…and dreaming.

Pure torture.

Sweet agony.

"Nope," she said and rubbed her tummy. "I'm full to the brim. You go ahead."

Josh swallowed hard and held his breath as she lifted her arms to stretch and a tiny strip of skin showed between the T-shirt and her waistband. Holy crap. The last slice of pizza would go untouched.

Don't look. Don't keep staring at that promise of satin smoothness. He breathed deep and then wished to hell he hadn't.

The torment of her sexy, clean scent in this small motel room kept reminding him of what his body desperately craved, what he hungered for beyond all reason. Just tossing her on the bed and losing himself in her and in the moment. They both could stand a release of their tension and of the tight muscles caused by the long flight. But being with her wouldn't be simple. If he so much as touched her now—there would be no way he could let her go.

Madness reigned.

Even the act of considering sex with Clare was pure madness.

"So how are we going to deal with the sleeping arrangements for tonight?" she asked behind a yawn.

He kicked his chair backward, stood and turned away so he wouldn't have to face all that temptation. "It's not something we need deal with. I don't intend to sleep. I'm the security. I do the bodyguarding. You do the sleeping." Opening his bag, he first checked the weapon they'd obtained earlier then pulled out an old T-shirt and a pair of running shorts.

"What? But you have to sleep. You'll be worthless tomorrow if you don't get your rest."

Turning back to her, Josh chanced a wry smile. "Sugar, there were lots of nights in the 'Stan when sleeping would've gotten me killed. Since I've been back, an hour or two is the most I need at night."

"You've never talked much about your time in the Rangers. You were injured in Afghanistan, weren't you?"

This was definitely not a topic he wanted to discuss right now. On the other hand, maybe it beat talking about sleeping arrangements.

He kept the T-shirt and shorts in his hands and sat back down in the chair by the table, leaning forward on his elbows and staring at the floor. "Yeah, I was injured." He raised his head, and then ratcheted his eyebrows up and down while he gave her his best grin. "But you should see the other guy."

Clare didn't laugh. She didn't even smile at the joke or his funny face as he'd hoped she would.

"How bad was it?" Her words were soft, tentative. Her eyes searched his for emotions he'd bet she didn't really want to see. "Were you shot? Or in one of those roadside explosions?"

He began to shake his head, fighting the deadly images, trying to come up with another joke or any other way out. But he couldn't find an alternative to giving her at least a partial explanation.

"I have nightmares about it sometimes," he admitted. Josh had never spoken to anyone about his nightmares and decided that reality would be a better choice for now. "We arrived at the drop zone in Black Hawks, as usual. Had to hit the ground in the middle of a swirling sandstorm caused by the bird's rotors—also as usual.

"My squad… We made our way to the target point behind a sandstone spire above a bluff about a quarter mile away. We were to be employed as spotters for a special-op bombing against a pocket of Taliban, supposedly located in the tiny village of Asmar in the Konar province. Our orders were to rendezvous with the AMF, the Afghan Militia. But before we could get there, the squad ran into resistance on the mountain trail."

In Josh's mind's eye he saw himself dragging his buddy Rodriguez through the firestorm of RPG rounds, finding a hidey-hole in the craggy rocks and dropping them both into it. Hell. The world had suddenly turned to a sandy, rocky hell all around them.

"Afterward, we learned a traitorous AMF squad turned us in to al-Qaeda. They pinned us down using the same GPS units that we were carrying in order to call in our bombers."

"GPS?" Attentive, Clare captured and processed every word. "You mean a Global Positioning System like the ones in cars that can give you a satellite road map?"

"Definitely. Made special for the army in microchip form so they can be carried around in your pocket or in your Jeep so you know where in the world you are."

She nodded and waited for him to finish.

Could he finish? Could he say the words? Could he possibly tell her that he had been tempted to use his grandmother's magic to cast a life spell around himself and Rodriguez? That he'd been tempted, but not convinced—not in time.

"A buddy and I were hit by sniper fire." The words fell from his mouth unbidden. "I made it out—in several pieces. He didn't."

Josh would never forget the look of shock on Rodriguez's face when the guy realized he'd been mortally wounded. That the blood pouring from his shoulder in thick red rivers flowed too freely…and carried the rest of his life with it. Too fast. No medic could've saved him. It had been too late for even the magic to save him. A chill swept through him as he clearly saw the past in his mind.

"It wasn't your fault," Clare told him with conviction. "It wasn't. A thing like that, done by traitors. During war time. You can't think you could've changed anything."

His body turned hard, cold. Sweat beaded on his forehead despite the room air conditioner laboring away behind them.

Abruptly, Josh stood and stalked toward the bathroom. "Go to bed," he muttered over his shoulder. "I'm grabbing a shower, then standing watch. I'll see you in the morning."

Dark shadows surrounded her with cloying, murky fear. Where was her child? Afraid to open her mouth, but more afraid not to, Clare called out. Her baby must be nearby, but why couldn't she hear him?

With sudden force, arms groped for her in the night. Next they roughly shoved her backward. Wait! Ow! Stop!

What about her son?

The shoving grew stronger. More urgent and insistent. Tripping over her own feet, Clare fell. Spiraling downward, she crashed past something that felt like a doorway and bumped into hidden objects in the dark on the way to the floor, landing on her knees in the dark.

Now her child's cries reached her ears, coming from somewhere straight ahead. Stumbling to her feet, Clare ignored the dizziness and her sudden shivering as she reached shaky hands out in front of her body. Fumbling frantically in the closed-in darkness, her only thought was to find her child.

The baby's cries turned mewling, begging for attention.

Crying for comfort. Needing his mother. The sound broke Clare's heart and spurred her into reckless action.

"I'm coming. Mommy's coming. Please don't cry."

She hit a wall to the left, spun, hit another wall to the right. After turning back the way she'd entered, she found the door locked behind her. Locked into some kind of closet? She trembled as an ominous and threatening panic surrounded her in veiled mists of pure hysteria. While she beat her fists against wood and wall, the claustrophobia crawled up her spine, grabbed her by the neck and squeezed.

No. Not now. She needed to think. To act.

To breathe!

"Let me out!" The words slipped past her throat in dry, raspy tones.

Why was everything so vague? Puzzling. Secretive.

And still the crying continued.

Frantic now, she shoved her shoulder against the hard mass of the door. At the last second it gave way and she fell again, this time into a murky light.

Another set of hands reached down and took her by the shoulder. "Let me help," the masculine voice said as he lifted her up. "I have the secret. Just say the word and your child will be saved."

Oh, thank heaven. A hero. But when she looked up into the shadowed face hovering above her, all she saw were the eyes— glowing red, sinister and wicked.

"No. Get away from me." She tried to break free from his grasp, but spiderwebs appeared, capturing her tightly in their gossamer tentacles and holding her by the man's side. Tangled up, she was pressed close to the stranger. Too close. She could feel his heat as his strong fingers continued to hold her by the shoulder.

And still the crying continued.

"Let me go!" She batted at the shadows surrounding the man's face and lunged backward trying to break free of his grip.

"Clare, hold on. Snap out of it. Let me help you." Josh's voice finally broke the spell of her dark dream.

She woke up crying, and saw him standing over her bed, grasping her shoulder with his tender touch. Chest heaving from the end of terror-filled sobs, Clare tried to catch her breath and fought to come fully awake.

"Oh God. I was dreaming." She shoved the hair from her eyes and tried to focus on her surroundings.

Josh turned on the low-wattage lamp beside the bed. "More like a nightmare, I'd say. Are you all right?"

"Yeah." After blinking away most of the dream's remnants, she took a good look at Josh and realized he was naked from the waist up. The jeans he'd been wearing had been replaced by a flimsy pair of running shorts. Clare sat straight up in bed and widened her eyes.

Suddenly she was noticing everything way too much. His hair hung down over his forehead and glistened with a wetness she would guess meant he'd recently stepped from the shower. The dark hair swirling across his naked chest glistened with moisture, too. Holy moly. Beneath the thick covering of silken hair lay strong chest muscles, rippling with tension as he stood transfixed and gazed into her face. Her glance roamed lower and landed on one of the world's top-ten flattest abdomens, marred only by an angry red scar running all the way from under an armpit to his waist.

Whew. Before her wandering gaze could go lower, she lifted her chin and met his eyes.

"What a terrible dream," she mumbled on a half sob. "I mean, Jimmy was lost—or maybe I was the lost one. Anyway, I couldn't find him in the dark, and then I got shoved into a kind of closet and couldn't find my way out. Couldn't get to the baby when he started crying. It was just awful."

"Shoved?" he asked warily. "Did you recognize anything? Or anyone?"

She shrugged a shoulder, then wrapped her arms around her waist and shivered. "Don't take this too literally, Josh. I was only dreaming. But anyway, I couldn't see much. Everything was cloaked and misty. Dark. But I felt an evil presence."

Josh eased himself down on the bed beside her and slipped an arm around her shoulders. "You're cold." He tugged her closer to his chest. "Is this better?"

Better? He had to be kidding. Now instead of chilled, her entire body was heating up beyond bearable.

"It was just a dream," she said again and tried to steady her breathing. "I'll come out of it soon."

"Do you think the dream might mean something? Could the evil presence have been your ex-husband?"

"I...don't know. I... For heaven's sake, who can tell anything by a dream?"

"My Mexican grandmother holds great store in dreams. She claims they can tell us things. What else do you remember?"

Clare closed her eyes and discovered impossible and fluctuating sensations in her belly. The dream hadn't quite let loose of her, yet the man sitting on the bed numbed her brain and caused butterflies to circulate in her body. Wanting to stand on her own and not lean on anyone too much, she struggled to make sense of her dreams and of her current thoughts. But the warmth of Josh's body blocked her best efforts.

"There was someone else there," she managed. "Someone I thought would protect my baby...but..."

Josh swung his feet up on the bed, still holding her close. "But what?"

"Nothing. Whoever or whatever it was all of a sudden turned

into something almost scary. Something—I don't know. Kind of wicked. Not evil exactly, but it made me nervous."

He chuckled. "That was some bad dream you had. My Grandmother Lupe would say it was foreshadowing your struggle, and then she'd tell you to prepare yourself for double trouble.

"But don't forget I'm here to protect you," he added gently. "And together you and I will keep Jimmy safe. I promise."

Clare figured she already had more than double the trouble, just sitting here with his scent and warmth surrounding her. She stopped thinking about the dream at all as their one spectacular kiss from this afternoon in Texas popped unbidden into her mind. She remembered back to the way he'd been teasing her with his tongue, and of how he'd let his hard arousal nestle against her belly. The very memory of what they'd done was causing her to experience sudden, heated dampness between her legs. Smoldering heat blossomed and skipped along her skin, prickling and tickling her in all the wrong places.

Ignoring self-preservation signals, both from her earlier dream and from her own common sense, Clare snuggled in closer to Josh. She felt an urgent pressure building to impossible heights inside her body and just let it take her.

Wanting him with a fierceness she'd never known, she pressed her lips to the center of his chest. He sucked in a whisper of breath and inched as far away as he possibly could and still be able to keep a steadying arm around her shoulders.

"I want you, Josh," she said in an amazingly breathless voice.

As close as she was to him, she couldn't help but notice when his pulse spiked at her words—and it amused her no end. She lifted her chin. Looking up into his eyes, she found the same desire there that she knew showed on her own face.

"We don't always get what we want, Clare," Josh told her with low and barely intelligible words.

"True. But I usually put my mind to whatever it is and plow

ahead anyway. And this time I will get what I need. I intend to have you tonight and consequences be damned. What do you think of that?"

"I think I need my head examined." With that he lowered his head and their lips met in a ferocious collision. Tongues tangled and bodies intertwined.

Tasting. Touching. Exploring.

Her hunger consumed her as their lips and arms and legs wound together. The next thing she knew, his calloused hands skimmed over her T-shirt and found her hard, aching nipples begging for his attention beneath the cloth.

She was having trouble breathing and wanted to feel the warmth of his fingers against her skin. As though he'd read her thoughts, Josh slid his hands up under her shirt and let his palms surround her breasts, lifting and caressing.

Kissing him hard on the mouth, Clare tried to put her whole body into the message she wanted him to receive. Urgent and demanding. *Stop thinking about tomorrow, Josh, please. And just take what's offered.*

In the very next moment, her body suddenly began screaming for release. Winding ever tighter and higher, she begged him silently to forget everything else for a few hours. Nothing mattered but their own needs. Not the nightmare. Not that she was a woman worried about a future. Not even motherhood mattered. Not right now.

For tonight, for just tonight, they could simply be together.

Running her fingers down his sinewy muscles, she felt her own blood pulsating deep inside, through veins and arteries. His lips moved in openmouthed hunger across her jawline and down her neck, while desire licked between them. Her nipples tightened in expectation.

She couldn't stand it another moment, so she ripped the T-shirt up over her head. His deep chuckle at her impatient move was so low and sexy she nearly fainted. Until...he bent to lave her wanting, waiting tips and lowered her back down on the bed.

He rolled over on top of her, positioning her where he wanted while continuing to tease and seduce. Toying with her breasts, he drove her crazy using teeth and a clever tongue. Her whole body arched into his mouth as she dug her fingers through his thick hair, holding him right where she wanted him.

Everything seemed fast and hot. So hot.

Why did he still have on his clothes? She wanted him. Right now.

Clutching at him, her fingers touched his flat abdomen and she felt the muscles there quiver under her assault. But that wasn't nearly enough. Sliding her fingertips under the waistband of his running shorts, she heard his breathing change over to short, sharp gasps.

"Easy there," he whispered hoarsely.

Clare tittered out a strangled laugh, so suddenly desperate and needy she thought she might explode. "No, not easy."

Tugging at his shorts, shoving at them, she pleaded for what she wanted. "Not a chance. I want it hard and I want it fast. And it has to be right now!"

Chapter 10

Josh sucked in a breath at Clare's words and reached for her wayward hand as she snuck it under the waistband of his running shorts. "Maybe we should…talk…about this."

Ignoring him and with fingers light and sweet, she clasped his erection. As she ran her hand down his slick hardness, his entire body stiffened in response. He swore under his breath.

"Don't think so," she said with a teasing giggle. Bending her head, she licked his nipple and then planted a sloppy kiss on his abdomen. "Tasting is better than talking any day. Yum."

A hiss leaked from between his parted lips. "Another minute and there won't be any going back."

It was already too late to stop what was happening between them. They both knew it. Gazing down at the vision of rapture on her face made him certain of their coming encounter. Her lips, swollen from his kiss. Her mussed hair. The drugged look In her eyes. He tried to steel himself against the raging fire of need as she moaned his name, but knew it was useless.

Breathing heavily, he reached down and took her wrist with firm resolve. "Unless your aim is to be done before we ever get started, let's slow things down." Pulling her hand upward, he pressed his lips to the center of her palm and watched as her eyes glazed with pleasure.

He needed to pleasure her. Needed to make everything right and memorable. Wanted to say with his body what he could never reveal to her in speech.

Holding her face between his hands, he took her mouth, kissing her as he had never kissed anyone before. He wanted to give her forever. But knew that was impossible. So he gave her whatever he had instead.

She arched into him, pleading silently. Insistently. In short order he did away with the final cloth boundaries between their bodies. Then he stopped, for just a moment, to revel in the exquisite form lying below him. When she began to squirm and moan under his perusal, he gave her what she wanted and moved his mouth over her shoulder blade, tasting the satin smoothness of her skin. The scent of her. The taste of her. How would he ever manage to put the erotic images and sounds she made back out of his mind again someday?

Still determined to do what was right for her, though, he followed his instincts and trailed butterfly kisses slowly downward, listening while her breathing became shallow and seductive. Soon his lips met the succulent channel between her breasts, and he tasted woman and desire in equal measure. He trailed a line downward, until his tongue found a new playground and ringed her navel. Josh had to set his mind to the effort of stemming his growing hunger. The urge to drive himself deep into her honeyed warmth was almost irresistible.

But being with her, watching the fire ignite in her eyes and breathing in the shimmering excitement as her own hunger built, was one of the most erotic and romantic things that had ever happened to him. Clare dug her heels into the bed and lifted her hips involuntarily. The sounds she made turned him to pure energy, like the blue flame. He cupped her bottom with his hands and gave in to the combustion.

Moving his mouth lower, he nipped at the nest of curls below her belly button. Teasing. Seducing. He planted soft kisses on the insides of her thighs and prayed for strength. His own breathing was loud in his ears and seemed spiked with lust. With a longing so strong he seethed with it, Josh spread her thighs open before him and nosed into the rosy bud of her core, swollen and damp and quivering with anticipation.

When Josh's hands began kneading her thighs, Clare curled her fingers into the sheets and held on. As his tongue and lips probed, licked and kissed her in a place that had never before been explored, she panted hard and fought to keep her hips still. But as hot sensations rippled right through her, from core to womb, she couldn't hang on, writhing and bucking and calling out his name.

Parting her own legs wider, she wanted more from him. More of those titillating and wanton shocks of pure ecstasy.

Josh obliged, caressing and licking, kissing and tormenting. Clare stopped breathing altogether. The first spasm jolted through her veins, surprising her like a lightning bolt out of the blue. Her whole body jerked as she shrieked in pleasure.

Josh never let up. Seducing her with his fingers, lips and tongue, he worked her tighter and higher. Her mind began to spin as psychedelic and neon colors whirled in kaleidoscope fashion behind her eyes. With her heart pounding triple-time inside her chest, she felt as though someone had knocked the breath right out of her. She couldn't...take...much...more.

Digging her fingers into his hair, she tugged him up her body and kissed him on the mouth. Her own taste was there on his lips, which made Clare go kind of nuts with untamed need.

"My turn," she mumbled and twisted her body so she could run her tongue down his abdomen—and lower still. At the same time, she dared to lightly trace the scar on his side and then to worship another deeper one on his upper thigh.

Nuzzling into hidden creases along his body, she tasted salty sweat and discovered she loved the course texture of the hair growing along the base of his shaft. Licking his erection and running her tongue up to the slick head, she fell in love with the tough, masculine feel of him.

A warrior lay beneath her. As she tasted and kissed to her heart's content, deep groans vibrated through him and into her. She moved her hands and began massaging his buttocks. Wanting to take all of him inside her body, she couldn't wait to fill herself with this man who had fought and survived in order to fight again for her sake.

Josh trembled and she sensed him nearing a ledge.

"Clare," he whispered almost reverently and rolled her to her back. "That's it. No more going slow."

Sliding her legs over his shoulders, Josh stared darkly into her eyes. "Stay with me." Then he plunged hard and deep, filling her up so far and fast that she gasped with the pure pleasure and shock of it.

Before she stopped seeing stars, he slowly backed out only to thrust in again. Ablaze with passion, her every nerve flamed as he repeated and repeated his slow assault.

Involuntarily she began moving as they set some ancient and primitive beat and she quickly matched his pace. This was basic. Wild and primal. Carnal and savage desire combusted between them but Josh never flinched or hesitated. His gaze held hers, hypnotizing her with a need so strong she felt bound to him by invisible steel bands. Together they went faster and faster. Climbed higher and higher.

Grabbing on to his arms in order to hang on, her mind went off the charts as she burned and sizzled. Everything ceased to matter but the two of them. In seconds, the pounding shock waves began in her toes and she convulsed as they rolled up along her body like an earthquake.

Josh captured her scream in his mouth, but still he drove into her. "Stay...." he breathed.

Hotter and higher he took her. Until her entire body quivered on the narrow precipice of a canyon filled with fire. Finally his body stiffened, and she bucked twice, digging her fingernails into his shoulders.

When his head reared back, he said her name like an oath as he poured himself into her. He collapsed, using his strong arms to enfold her body. His head nuzzled the hollow at the base of her neck.

Clare waited for her heart to start up again then pulled him close and kissed his forehead. "Well, that was fun. When can we do it again?"

She wanted to keep it light between them because the real truths to her feelings were dark and dangerous. Never before had sex meant so much. Was it love? Or was it just the most fantastic sex in the world?

Whatever it was, she didn't want to talk about it. Not right now. Maybe tomorrow when her pulse was back to normal and her heart wasn't so fragile.

Josh smiled against her neck and waited for his body to reassemble itself. His cellular structure had dissolved into one huge lump of panting, pulsating hormones with a twist of something he didn't recognize and couldn't name.

He tried to figure out what had just happened between them, knowing it was one of the most explosive and *the* most sensual encounters of his entire life. Lying there, the thought came to him that the last few minutes with Clare had literally taken him to somewhere past all his experience. To somewhere that was an escape from his regular world and from all the contradictions involved in this thing called his life. Their coming together had seemingly caused the world to spin them off into a dream world, or maybe into a solitary cocoon, all their own.

So now what? As his pulse slowed back to normal, he understood that in the morning life would go on. Of course he'd rather stay right here with her forever. But forever was beyond his control. He would be lucky to control the next few hours.

Finally able to command at least his limbs, he leaned up on one elbow and took a moment to look down on her. Just to gaze at the picture she made, with her heavy-lidded eyes and satisfied smile.

"Soon," he answered at last, but the word came out more like a huff.

She grinned and stretched, her movements stirring his obviously not-so-abused body back to life.

"Maybe very soon." He reached over and tucked a stray strand of silken hair behind her ear.

Her lids fluttered as she moaned and arched up to plant a kiss on his chin. "Mmm. Think we can keep this up indefinitely?"

For the moment Josh wanted to believe they could make a go of it for real. That indefinitely was possible. That there were no such things as witchcraft and curses and ex-husbands. And that tomorrow's sunrise would never come.

Flicking a thumbnail over her nipple and watching her squirm under his attention, Josh decided to pretend they could find forever together—even if only for the few hours left of tonight.

Later—maybe just a few minutes later, or maybe hours and hours later—Clare turned into Josh's arms again, breathing heavily and absolutely amazed at her own stamina. He was all the things she'd ever dreamed of as a girl and had come to decide didn't exist.

What they were doing wasn't wrong, she decided smugly. Letting this man ease her aches and fill the void—even if it would only be for a few stolen hours—could not be wrong. Not when it felt so right. Yes, she was a mother and wanted to be the best one she had the power to be. But she was also a woman with needs of her own. She hadn't even known how truly strong her needs could be.

Josh slid his hand up her arm and ever so slowly touched her sensitive breasts. Even after all these hours of making love with him, she shivered in response. They'd gone from wild and incandescent sex to sweet and mind-blowing passion.

Every minute—every instant—was elegant and spine-tingling.

With deliberate and slow moves he kept driving her to the next level. Higher and higher. He had her life, the beating of her heart and the blood coursing through her arteries, in the palm of his hand. And she'd never felt more vulnerable—or more powerful.

Suddenly a thought poked into her head about protection. Whoa. Just a little bit too late for that one, to be sure. Though she wasn't worried in the least about the health of either of them, what would they do if she got pregnant? Of course, Josh believed he was cursed and sterile, but Clare didn't consider such a thing in the realm of possibility.

Could she talk to him about it? She wanted to tell him everything, this man who was giving her so much. To say all the things she had never dared tell anyone. About wishing for a big family, which she knew was not a currently fashionable view. But having lots of kids had always been her dream and someday she would have it. Maybe tonight had been the first step in finding that dream. Wouldn't that be wonderful?

With that thought, she discovered herself wishing for something new. There was a new daddy featured in a prominent spot in her dream. More than just any daddy, the man who was already standing beside her in her quest to save her child. Josh. He'd managed to turn her dream from black-and-white to living color and she wanted him to live it with her.

But she hesitated to destroy the magic spell they were under tonight. That would be one very serious and maybe scary discussion. At least it would be if his sister had been right about him believing he couldn't have kids because of some family curse. So she kept her mouth shut and gave herself up to the moment.

Once she was free of worry about Jimmy, they could have their talk. Tonight? Well, tonight would be just for the magic.

"You okay? You went away there for a moment." Josh leaned closer and nipped at her bottom lip. His breath was shallow, hot and sweet and driving her right back into the conflagration.

She ran her hand down his body, loving the slightly sticky feel of the man who had sweated just to please her. "You can't get rid of me so easily, cowboy. I can keep up with you with no problem. Wanna try me?"

Without words Josh showed her how much he wanted to try. And true to her words, Clare kept up with him—no problem.

The next morning's rain came down in buckets. Staying in bed with Clare instead of getting up and going out for breakfast in the downpour didn't bother Josh in the least. There was a tiny two-cup coffeepot in their room and they brewed a pot before taking a shower together—which dissolved into a two-hour session that ended up back in bed.

But when the time came to leave for their appointment, Josh forced his mind into the moment while the two of them got dressed. On any special op, a Ranger knew better than to let his thoughts drift off into dreams of a special woman or to last night's warm bed. It could get him killed. So he'd learned how to block out any thoughts but of the mission.

Josh's mission here was protection, not getting it on with the protectee. Clare needed him to be clearheaded and focused on seeing her to the meeting with the man from the Justice Department and then back home again. He should've damned well kept his hands off her. But that was a load of guilt that could wait for another time. Right now it was time to face reality and be her bodyguard as he'd promised.

Picking up the Glock 9 mm, Josh checked the clip, chambered a round and wished to hell he had the heavier Colt .45 he'd requested instead of this lightweight, easy-to-jam piece of crap. Ah, hell. Any armament was better than none, he supposed.

Shoving the weapon in his waistband, Josh shrugged into his jacket and waited for Clare to finish brushing her hair. He stood at the front door with his arms crossed and gazed toward the open bathroom door where Clare was standing. She scowled into the tiny mirror as she dragged a brush through her sunflower-colored tangles.

Her brush moved in long, measured strokes, and Josh's mind wandered toward her slender neck and the soft slope of her shoulder. He remembered placing his lips just there at the base of her neck last night, and he immediately thought of the murmurs of pleasure he'd gotten for his trouble.

"Let's go," she said as she pitched the brush into her bag and started toward him.

He had to swallow down the stupidity of once again veering off into the fantasy of all the things they'd done together last night. Next up would be the tougher job of finding a way to hide the growing erection under his jeans zipper. Letting himself lose focus was dumb.

And dumb might be one thing, but stupid could just plain get them both killed. He drew in a breath and made himself over into smart.

Josh drove and Clare navigated through the busy, wet streets of the Capital. The rain had slowed to drips by the time they'd parked the rental car in a parking garage on K Street and walked over to the pub on Pennsylvania. Because of the drizzle, they were able to snag an outside table under the awning. Josh eased onto a chair with his back to the wall, a position where he had the best view of the street. He guided Clare into the seat next to him where she could see anyone going by, too.

"How are we supposed to recognize this guy?" he asked.

She shrugged. "Not sure. Maybe we'll just watch out for a single man who seems to be looking for someone."

This wasn't the most well-thought-out part of their whole plan, and Josh couldn't wait to tease Maggie about screwing up when they got home. But at this point they had little choice but to roll with it.

"Before he arrives," Josh began soberly. "I want you to go over the plan again. Remember…"

"Yes, I know," she interrupted. "Under no circumstances am I to call you by your real name. I'm to do all the talking and introduce you as my cousin Albert."

Josh winced at the name, but nodded his head. "Right. When he gets here, I will excuse myself and then stand back where he can't see me, but where I can see and hear everything that's going on." Josh vowed to keep his eyes open and trained on their surroundings, and to have his weapon ready at all times.

They ordered nachos and beer and watched as people began dashing through the raindrops and into the pub for an early lunch. Just as their order arrived, a solitary man in a gray tweed suit got out of a cab and slowly moved toward them under the canopy.

"Mrs. Al-Hamzah?"

Clare's face turned deeply crimson as she stood. "The name's Clare Chandler," she corrected. "My husband and I are divorced. And I assume you are Roger Wilkins of Justice."

"Yes, ma'am."

"Fine." She turned toward Josh, who stood beside her. "This is my cousin Albert. He was kind enough to accompany me today, but he has a call to make."

Josh shook the man's hand then excused himself. He'd already scouted out a good vantage point behind the open glass door that led to the vestibule. While the Justice Department man ordered food, Josh scanned the street and then took a quick glance at the tables just inside the pub. He didn't like what he saw. There were too many people, both in the pub and on the street. Cars crawled by and the strangers inside them gawked over at those crazy people sitting outside the pub in the rain.

He knew Maggie and Ethan had wanted them to be out in the open and in public for this meeting, but he felt too exposed here. Why the hell couldn't Clare have just phoned this man? Then they could be safe and sound back in Texas where he knew his way around.

Cursing silently, Josh recounted how both Clare and Ethan convinced him she needed to come to Washington in person. That her presence could make the whole difference as to whether the Justice Department would take her case or not.

Well, fine. Slinking back into the shadows, Josh moved his hand behind his back and let it hover over the weapon as he eavesdropped on Clare and the Justice man.

After Mr. Wilkins ordered, Clare began the short speech she'd prepared. She told him of her predicament and of how her son needed his mother. Going a little further than she'd planned, Clare also went into all the reasons she felt her son should be allowed to enjoy the advantages of becoming an American, as was his birthright. She talked for so long her throat was dry.

Mr Wilkins finally looked up from his food and cut her off. "I know your reasons are valid, Ms. Chandler. I can appreciate your situation. And more to the point, you have the Constitution and laws on your side. But…"

"But what? What don't I know?"

He sighed heavily. "I did a little checking after your friend contacted me. Unfortunately, you've stepped right smack into the middle of a sensitive political hornet's nest."

"What are you talking about? How can a mother and her child be anything but the plain and simple way nature intended things to be?"

"*Oil*, ma'am." Mr. Wilkins set his water glass down and looked her straight in the eyes. "There's a highly classified and delicate negotiation going on with the Abu Fujarah government as we speak. No one on our side can afford to go against the sheikh right now."

He took a breath and continued. "It's a diplomatic nightmare at the moment. Maybe next year, after the treaties are settled, we can help you."

"Next year?" Clare heard the hysteria mounting in her voice as the words sounded more like shrieking. "What am I supposed to do in the meantime?"

"Maybe you should take the baby back for now. Just until—"

"No way." Her mind was racing. How could things be so messed up?

"I hate to say this, Ms. Chandler, but you may not have a choice. There's a rumor being circulated over at State that shortly you may become a wanted woman."

"Wanted? For what?" Her tones had shot up into the screaming range, but she couldn't help it.

The poor man across from her winced but hung in there. "I'm afraid a warrant is probably imminent, ma'am. I understand it will be issued against you for kidnapping one baby Prince Bashshar al-Hamzah."

Kidnapping! Her own son? Oh. My. God.

Chapter 11

Josh stepped out of the shadows, reached into his pocket and threw a wad of twenties on the table. Without a word, he took Clare's elbow and lifted her to her feet.

"Take your time over lunch, pal," he told the man from Justice. "It's been real."

Clare's eyes were wide but she never balked and didn't open her mouth. She marched beside him as they headed in the opposite direction from where they'd left the rental car.

Down the block, she turned to him. "Did you hear that, Josh? They're saying I kidnapped Jimmy." The soft sob at the end of her sentence could barely be heard, but it was there nevertheless.

Josh's gut clenched. He wondered what it was about Clare that had gotten to him so easily. Why in only a few days' time would he sooner die than see her and her son separated. And just the thought of her landing in jail because she wanted to keep her son... Well, hell. Not while he was alive and kickin'.

"I heard." He'd stepped up their pace and now was nearly dragging her along the sidewalk behind him.

"Where are we going?"

"Back to the rental car. The long way 'round."

"But…"

He turned the next corner and found himself in the college area of Foggy Bottom. "Can you keep up, please? We need to lose anyone who might be following."

She hesitated for only a second, apparently stunned at the thought of someone watching them. But then she got herself in gear and matched every one of his steps with two of her own.

Crossing the street, he turned back and hoped to cloak their movements by joining a crowd of young people waiting to cross the street in the other direction. Bless Clare, she kept up and never questioned.

In silence, they crossed over and switched back and forth for the next twenty minutes. Both of them were breathing heavy when they finally entered the parking garage.

"You really think someone was following us?" she asked between her panting breaths.

"Maybe—probably." He let her into the car, buckled himself up and started the engine. "Hopefully we lost them."

"What if we didn't? What if…what if they're still around?"

He smiled at her, hoping to ease her fears. "Well now," he began, putting a Texas twang into the words for effect. "This here rental ain't Lucille, but she'll do. Let's just take one step at a time."

Whether it was his certain tone or maybe the exaggerated twang, something made her smile over at him as she buckled her seat belt. That beam of a smile brightened up the drizzly gray day and almost made him forget their predicament. Almost.

Pulling out into the city traffic, Josh's brain was whirling. What direction should he drive? To the motel? To the airport? Nowhere sounded very good if they had picked up a tail.

Josh decided the airport in Baltimore would be their best course. As busy at it was there, they could surely lose any tail.

"Get the map and find the shortest way to reach the Baltimore airport, will you?" Keeping Clare busy had another use. It would keep her mind off her problems for a little while longer.

She dug out the map and spent a few minutes orienting herself. Meanwhile, Josh just drove the streets and watched the rearview mirror. Taking a look out the windshield, Clare pointed out the proper street to take them closest to the Interstate. Breathing a little easier once they were on the 395, Josh relaxed into the fast city driving the best way he could.

"So, is it Ramzi's men we're trying to avoid? Or…or the cops? After all, I could be a wanted woman."

He heard the near hysteria in her voice and tried to think of some way of calming her down. Truthfully, he wasn't feeling all that steady himself.

"We're not running from anyone, sugar. We're just making our way back home. We'll talk about the future and your choices when we get to Texas."

Clare heaved a deep sigh, then turned her face to look out her window. "I miss Jimmy," she said so quietly he almost didn't hear her. "You don't think he's forgotten me, do you?"

"We haven't even been gone for twenty-four hours. He's not likely to forget his mama so soon."

She sniffed and kept her face turned away.

Josh threaded his way through the heavy traffic but kept one eye on Clare. It broke his heart not being able to tell her that things would all work out in the end. He wanted to wrap her and Jimmy up in his arms and keep them safe and sound for good. But he just didn't see how that could ever work.

Too many problems. First and foremost, the problem of him not being able to have children. Insurmountable. Then there was the problem of Ramzi eventually finding them. And he would.

But before even that, Clare might be forced to hire an attorney to keep herself out of jail. And what would become of Jimmy then? If Josh didn't miss his guess, the minute Ramzi found out where Jimmy was he would have him on a plane headed back to the Middle East before any of them could stop him.

Hell.

Checking the rearview mirror again, Josh nearly choked when he noticed a big SUV, a Hummer, shoving into the line of traffic behind them. He tried to think, to remember Ethan's instructions. Weaving to the left, he crossed three lanes of traffic to the fast lane and stepped on the gas, hoping the big SUV wouldn't keep up. Hoping it wasn't really following them.

No such luck. The Hummer crossed over and moved in behind him. Josh varied his speed, slowing and speeding up randomly. Still the Hummer hugged his bumper.

Luckily, a line of three semi-tractor-trailers was coming up fast to his right. Josh cut in front of the first one and watched in his rear mirror as the truck driver shot him the finger. Sorry, bud, but you're the only hope we've got.

"What's going on?" Clare's eyes were still damp when she turned to question him.

"Somebody's on our tail."

She cranked her head around and looked through the back window. "Where? Can we lose them?"

"The navy-blue Hummer on our left. And we're going to give it our best try. Hang on."

Taking a deep breath, he shot to the right and snuck into the middle of a long line of cars. He saw what he needed dead ahead and jerked hard right on the wheel again, careening off an exit ramp. Stomping on the brake, Josh slowed enough to make the light at the bottom of the ramp. In seconds it turned green and he shot left and then left again as he pushed the little rental in a double-back move.

"We're going south now," Clare complained as they took the ramp back onto the Interstate. "Away from the airport."

Josh swallowed hard and kept checking his rearview mirror as he joined the southbound traffic and moderated his speed to match theirs. "For a while. I want to get away from the hub of the city and then stop at a gas station or convenience store. We need to call Ethan."

With the heavy traffic, it took them a good half an hour to drive into the suburbs. But there had been no sign of the navy Hummer since Josh had made his maneuver on the interstate. They stopped at a convenience store on a corner, and Josh pulled out the cell to call his brother.

On shaky legs, Clare headed inside to look for a restroom. Josh had done an amazing job of losing the bad guys. But she needed a moment to recuperate.

Splashing cold water on her overheated face, she stared at her splotchy cheeks and red-rimmed eyes. Oh, nice. But at least she was still alive and free, and shortly she would be heading back to see her son. At least, she hoped to be on an airplane soon—and not in jail.

On a halfhearted attempt, she tried to tame her hair but soon gave up in frustration. Swinging back out of the bathroom, she nosed into the coolers looking for bottled water. But the instant she'd entered the store proper, the room had darkened like a storm cloud moving in to cover the fluorescent lights. The place was packed with people all shopping and chatting, but Clare felt sure someone somewhere watched her every movement.

Where was this spooky feeling coming from? She shoved open a wall cooler, searching for the right size water, but had to stop and check over her shoulder. Too many people for her to judge who might be watching her. But this icy chill down her spine was not coming from the air-conditioned drink cooler.

A man crowding in beside her frowned when she kept standing in his way. "Oh. Sorry." She stepped aside, but he knocked into her as he grabbed for a drink.

Rude man. When he was gone, she pulled out two waters and headed for the cashier. Still the itchy feeling of being watched permeated her entire being.

The crowd at the cashier's counter was thick. Sweaty bodies surrounded her and little kids shoved past everyone else, looking at the low shelves with the candy. Her paranoia and claustrophobia built to where she couldn't wait to get back outside to Josh and the rental car. Just in time, she reached the cashier, paid for the waters and dashed out the glass door.

Free. Safe.

But instead of those sun-filled emotions, the bad feelings of paranoia followed her right out to the parking lot. But where…

She hadn't taken fifteen steps across the parking lot toward Josh when all of sudden she looked up and realized a tight circle of men surrounded her, closing in. Uh-oh. It wasn't paranoia if someone really was after you.

Taking a breath, she tried to judge if these men were the police or if they were Ramzi's men again. There wasn't much of a chance to decide. If she was going to do anything to help herself, it had to be now.

Clare let out the loudest screech she could manage and then grabbed her foot and began hopping away. People all around turned to look and a couple of them came toward her out of concern. One of the scary big guys in the circle tried to stop her, laying a firm hand on her shoulder.

But by then, another man had come over to see what the problem was. "Hey, you okay?"

Clare figured this was it. If these men were the police, they would have to identify themselves right now. Instead, the big guy dropped his hand and stepped away.

Right. "Sorry for the scare," she told the concerned stranger. "I just twisted my ankle."

"Clare." Josh pushed his way past the crowd.

When he saw the problem and Clare bent over rubbing her ankle, he swung her up in his arms. "Let's get you to the car." He turned to the concerned stranger. "Thanks. But I've got her now."

The crowd began to disperse. Josh lightly set her down in the passenger seat and then jumped to the driver's side. Thirty seconds later they were pulling out onto the four-lane road in front of the store.

"What happened?" He stepped on the gas as he spoke and kept an eye on his rearview mirror.

Her heart was still racing, her breathing still coming in gasps. "I thought I could feel someone watching me in the store. Then when I came out, four big guys surrounded me. Scared me to death."

"So you screamed?"

"It was the best I could think of at the time."

"Smart. It worked."

His approval meant more to her than it should. "Thanks." The grin across her face had moved right from her heart. "But what are we going to do?"

"I called Ethan. He's in D.C. already. We're going to meet him at the mall and change cars. That should throw them off."

But in that instant, it became clear that they weren't going to make it to the mall. A black Explorer came up fast on their left and boxed them in. The navy Hummer from earlier pulled in directly behind them, and a couple more SUVs drove in formation behind that. Clare stiffened and tried to keep breathing.

"What now?"

Without answering, Josh twisted the wheel and tore down a side street to the right. The squeal of tires and the grinding sounds of heavy cars shifting gears ran through the air. Josh stepped on it, but they found themselves racing down a residential street.

Trees and houses. Sidewalks and kids' toys. Speeding down these streets would be too dangerous.

"Slow down," Clare yelled when she spotted a kid on a bike. She grabbed hold of her door's armrest and held her breath.

Josh turned right at the next corner. He didn't know what to do or where to hide. In another block, he found himself driving the boundary road of a city park. Maybe he could lose them there.

He couldn't see any of the SUVs but almost felt the bad guys sniffing them out and closing in around them. This park just had to be their salvation. Spotting a one-lane side road into the park that was surrounded by trees and nearly hidden, Josh turned onto it and slowed way down. At this low speed maybe the bad guys wouldn't be able to hear his engine.

Checking his mirror again, he lightly stepped on the brake and came to a crawl.

"Josh, watch out!"

When he jerked his gaze back around to the windshield, he realized he'd driven the rental car into a dead end. A few feet in front of them stood a locked fence gate with a sign that read Private. No Trespassing.

Hell.

No choice but to turn around. He threw the transmission into Reverse and dragged on the wheel. But before he managed the full one-eighty, the Hummer came around a corner on the one-lane road behind them and slowed to a stop. It stood in their way, heaving and rumbling like a live beast.

"What'll we do?" Clare's voice was two octaves higher than normal.

His whole body on alert, Josh reached into his waistband and pulled out the Glock. "Let's see if we can bluff our way out. Stay put."

Throwing the car into Park, he left the motor running and stepped outside the driver's door. Leaving the open door between himself and the Hummer, Josh drew a bead directly between the eyes of the front passenger who was talking on a cell phone. Josh wasn't totally stupid.

"What do you want?" As he called out to them, he saw both the passenger and the driver opening their eyes wide at the sight of the Glock.

After a slight exchange between the two men, the passenger dropped his phone and opened his door to get out. "Clare Chandler," the man called out from a spot of safety behind his own door. "His Excellency Abdullah Ramzi al-Hamzah wishes to speak to you. We are not here to harm you, only to take you there to talk."

"Josh," Clare whispered. "Maybe I should go with them. I won't tell him where Jimmy is. What can he do to me?"

"Stay put," he ordered. "Slide down in the seat so you're not so much of a target."

"But…"

"Do it."

Josh heard her sighing heavily, but she inched her way down in the seat until she was nearly sitting on the floor mats.

"It's not going to happen, fellas. Tell your boss that Ms. Chandler has nothing to say."

The man standing beside the Hummer ducked his head inside the front seat, pulled out a mini-Uzi submachine gun and pointed it at Josh. "We have no quarrel with you, and no wish to do you harm. But the woman goes with us."

Josh sighted and readied his gun. "Back off. We're leaving. Move out of the way now."

A staccato rat-a-tat resounded in the late-afternoon air as the man released a round from the Uzi as a warning. Clare squeaked and covered her eyes.

"First rule. Never fire unless you mean it," Josh said under his breath.

And he meant it. A trained soldier always shot to kill. Josh pulled the trigger on the Glock; the man dropped to the ground. The Uzi went flying. At that moment, the driver slammed the Hummer into Reverse and sped off backward down the lane, with the passenger door flapping open and his comrade lying face-down on the pavement.

Josh dove into the rental and finished turning it around. Clare blinked frantically and nearly hyperventilated as he maneuvered the car around the body.

"Ohmygod. Ohmygod. We're going to die."

"Buckle up. We're not dying yet. But we've got to get outta here," he told her.

He sped down the lane half expecting to run into the Hummer blocking the way. But the way out was clean. Shadows of sunset had begun to conceal the roadways as Josh fought his jackhammering heart and drove the speed limit back out to the interstate.

"Was that man dead?" Clare's face was pale and her whole body shook.

"I don't know. Maybe." It wouldn't be the first time Josh had been forced to kill someone. But each time it had been either his own life or theirs. That wasn't where the guilt lay. No, the real guilt was in not saving the people who'd counted on him. This time, he vowed that Clare would not be one of those mistakes.

Not on my watch. Roger that.

"No, sir, Your Excellency," the private investigator told Ramzi. "Our man Mohammed Yusuf did not receive a fatal wound. He needed many sutures in the scalp and will rest for a few days. But he is merely embarrassed."

"He should be fired." Ramzi's blood pressure was skyrocketing, yet he spoke with low and measured tones. "My orders were not to hurt anyone. Why did he feel that shooting off a weapon was within his right?"

The private investigator looked sheepish, which only served to make Ramzi hotter. "The baby was not with the woman. We made sure of that. The woman would not come with us willingly. She has an armed protector. We did execute our secondary plan, but I apologize…"

Ramzi was on his feet instantly. "Shut up, you asinine idiot. I asked you to bring her here if my child could not be found. I did not expect you to kidnap her at gunpoint.

"If she had been killed, I might never have found the prince." Ramzi's nerves were frayed. This whole mess with Clare was beginning to tell on him.

His father had sent word that he would be coming to America in a few days. Ramzi was well aware that the oil treaty would be his father's main reason to travel all this way. But his father would expect to hear good news about his grandson when he arrived. He would expect to *see* his grandson.

It was time for Ramzi to take charge of this investigation. He needed his son. Whatever it took.

Chapter 12

"So, was the guy dead or not?" Ethan stood beside his Toyota hybrid, dangling the car keys in his hand.

Josh shrugged a shoulder. "We didn't stick around to find out." He kept one hand on the open door and the other held out for the keys.

"I'll have a friend check into it and let you know. Meanwhile, I've got a contact in State who can keep us up to date on Clare's status." Ethan switched keys with him. "You and Clare have the directions to the Baltimore airport by the back way, don't you?"

Josh ducked his head and checked with Clare, who was already buckled into the passenger seat. "We're all set, right, navigator?"

Clare nodded but didn't say anything. Worry over her emotional state had begun to hamper Josh's discussion with Ethan. He needed her to remain alert. They had only one more security check before they could get back to Texas, but it was important to handle it right. She needed to stay centered and determined. All would be lost if she gave in to panic.

Ethan reminded him of where to park the hybrid so the car could be found at the airport later. After gripping Josh's shoulder for a momentary show of solidarity, his brother climbed into the rental and took off. Josh slid behind the wheel of the hybrid and buckled up.

"You okay?"

Clare turned. Her eyes were glazed over and she looked a little shaky. "I...don't know. That man can't be dead. He just can't be."

Josh took her hand. The electric jolts from their joined fingers stunned him for a second. They'd been so busy surviving the bad guys, he hadn't had a chance to consider their one spectacular night, or to dwell on how their bodies had just seemed to belong locked together. How right that had felt. His gut tightened when images of all they'd done flicked into his mind, but his concern for her tamped down the physical response.

He lifted her fingers to his lips and tenderly kissed each tip. Clare blinked and her eyes widened. Her cheeks turned pink as she stared up at their hands, wound together at his mouth. He liked that color in her face a lot better than the wan look of a second ago.

Using his other hand, he reached over and teased her lips with his thumb pad. A low groan vibrated through her whole body, so he let his thumb linger, rubbing her bottom lip. She opened her mouth and sucked his finger inside, tonguing and mimicking what she wanted them to do together. He couldn't stop the pull running from his fingers to his hard arousal as a smoldering heat darkened her gaze. Hell, he wasn't so sure he even wanted to stop.

Sweet mercy. She *was* in shock. This wasn't like her.

Josh eased his thumb out of her mouth, turned and, sighing, cranked the engine to life. "You and Jimmy are going to be just fine, Clare. This change of cars with Ethan will keep our whereabouts hidden until we can board the plane. But if we continue sitting here for another couple of minutes like this, the two of us are likely to get ourselves arrested."

"Do you think I care?" she snapped. "I could be arrested at any moment anyway."

When he turned to check on her, he thanked God the anger sparked from her astoundingly golden eyes. She was one extraordinary woman. Gorgeous and resilient. A real mother bear protecting her young, and so sensual a man could lose his ever-loving mind just looking at her. And instead of shaky and frightened, for the moment, this woman of his dreams was downright mad. Anger would keep her sharp.

He prayed for the strength to keep her safe. To see her and Jimmy happy together in their own place. And he prayed for his sorry-ass self, too, knowing he would have to walk away when it was done.

He did not belong with her, even though their bodies shouted that they were meant for each other every single time they came close enough to touch.

Leaving the car in Neutral and his foot on the brake, Josh forgot his wariness for the moment and leaned over to take her mouth in a sizzling blast of heat and feeling. He put his heart into making love to her lips. He put his whole spirit behind showing her just how he felt through only a kiss. Then he promised her nothing but goodbye as he broke it off and straightened up.

"When we get to the airport, I'll call Maggie. She'll have a plan B drawn up by now. Don't worry." It would be great if he could follow his own advice and stop worrying, too, but chances of that were not likely.

Though one thing rang true. He knew it as well as he knew a clear Texas sky. "You're not going to jail and your ex will not take Jimmy away. None of us is going to let that happen."

With his determination to see her safely on her way cracking under the pressure of losing her, Josh threw the hybrid's transmission into Drive and headed toward the airport—and their last few hours together.

They wore sunglasses and ball caps through their entire wait time at the airport, and made it past security with no trouble. The minute they took their seats on the flight, Clare closed her eyes and fell sound asleep, leaving Josh alone to weigh everything that had happened and to tick off what steps they needed to take to make it safely home.

When he'd talked to Maggie on the phone before the flight, she'd said she would tell Clare her new plan in person, and then she'd advised him to fly a roundabout route. So they were on a flight bound for Kansas City. From there they would go to Denver and then Dallas before boarding a flight for San Antonio. It was a smart plan, but Josh still felt something, some small precaution maybe, had not been considered.

He fidgeted in the narrow seat. His gut was churning, his instincts raw and on edge.

Deciding to stretch his legs, Josh stood and straightened, kicking out the kinks. When he looked up the aisle at all the faces of the other people on their flight as they relaxed in their seats, it finally occurred to him to wonder what he would do if he were in the same position as Clare's ex and wanted *his* child back. Kidnap Clare and demand that she tell him where the boy was? Not if her ex knew Clare at all.

Clare would never give up her baby. Not a chance in the world. So if Josh were an ex-husband looking for his son, he would find a way of following Clare until she led him back to Jimmy. Looking again at their fellow passengers, Josh wondered if perhaps any of these people was one of the bad guys and had followed them. But how would he know if they were?

Slowly walking the center aisle, Josh studied every face. Or at least those that weren't buried in a magazine or book. After every few steps he took, the atmosphere in the cabin changed. Not the air pressure. Not even the altitude. No, this change felt more along the lines of atmospheric *impressions.*

God, where had his subconscious dug up that word? He hadn't heard it or used it in… Well, not since before his mother died.

But that word fit what was happening to him. When he strolled past one particular face or another, his mind would crackle with images. Images of those people's lives, and worse yet, their feelings. Nothing this exotic had happened to him since he'd been a kid.

Yeah, and back then he had buried the ability. Buried it so deep, he'd actually forgotten altogether. Could he retrieve the power now? Now that those senses might really come in handy?

Josh strolled down the aisle, trying to soak in all the mind pictures he was receiving. But there were so many images that the jumble became shattered and confusing. Had he lost the capacity to use his inherited power? It'd never occurred to him, back when he was cursing his abilities and wishing for a different parentage, that he might ever need to read people's…well, not exactly their minds, more like their dreams and desires. But at this moment, that's exactly what he needed to do. Hell.

Running his hands through his hair in frustration, Josh went back to his seat. He wanted to think over this whole problem some more. Try to sort out his own tumbled emotions.

It seemed as if his entire life had been geared toward stepping away from the witchcraft, and away from the odd powers he'd always dreaded. So now he had a lot of questions for himself. Why change everything he believed in at this stage? Why give up every concept he'd held dear?

Witchcraft was nonsense. Normal people didn't believe in it.

Glancing over at a sleeping Clare, Josh thought of what might happen to her and Jimmy if he failed to help them escape. His chest hurt and he broke into a sweat as the first image of her losing her son came into his mind. And that told him his answer.

If she was important enough to lose his life over—and he'd been ready and willing to do exactly that back at the suburban park—if her situation was urgent enough to face a Hummer and the bad guy with an Uzi, then it was certainly important enough to change his worthless ideas about witchcraft.

Jimmy was important enough. Clare was definitely important enough. Son of a gun. *He loved them both.*

Clare leaned her seat back to the reclining position and tried to get her mind off the rugged loner sleeping in the seat next to her. Josh Ryan was a puzzle and trying to fit the pieces together was driving her to distraction. She'd already tried sleeping and managed only a couple of hours on the first leg of their journey. Then she'd tried reading. She'd even tried making conversation with a woman who'd sat to the opposite side of her on their way to Denver. But nothing had worked.

The one image clogging her mind, and that kept her on the edge of her seat and on the verge of a breakdown, was how she'd nearly lost him. The thought of how close he'd come to taking a bullet for her back there in Washington threw her into a depression so deep it threatened to drown her in a blue funk.

So far she'd managed a truly magnificent job of avoiding all thoughts of what the two of them had done last night. Of what their lovemaking and his tender attentions had meant to her. Though, really, after she'd found out she might be wanted for kidnapping her own son, it had been easy enough to push those thoughts aside and call it just great—no, make that the best— sex of her entire life.

But dear Lord. The man had stood up for her in the face of a submachine gun. He could have killed another human being in order to keep her safe.

What would she have done if Josh himself had been shot and…killed?

The idea made her sick to her stomach. She glanced over at him, slouched uncomfortably in the narrow seat. His chin, which last night she had discovered tasted like an erotic citrus-scented lollipop, was turning dark with afternoon stubble. His six-pack abs remained flat and touchable even as he slumped. Her thoughts turned to running her fingers down that abdomen and then exploring the territory below. But she remembered where they were in time and interrupted those thoughts by staring at his long, lean legs, stretched forward and stuck out dangerously into the aisle. The man was beautiful in a rugged, masculine way.

And he was everything she'd ever dreamed of in a partner for life. So much more than she'd ever hoped to find. So much more than she deserved.

Last night had been real and immediate. For both of them. Today, facing that gun had been *too* real. What would tomorrow bring?

A rude awakening to the truth of reality, that's what. Reality to the fact that she still needed to run away and hide out from Ramzi. Maybe for the rest of her son's childhood years.

She turned her head away from the sight of the dearest man besides her father that she'd ever known. If she'd had the time to work on it, she might have been able to convince Josh to build a family with her—to love her.

He had made himself into a loner because of his guilt, and he'd convinced himself that a convenient curse would keep him from putting down roots. Nevertheless, he did have a family who cared about him and a place where he belonged. She wouldn't be able to go back to her home. And she wouldn't have a shot at talking Josh into making a family with her. There would be no big family with tons of kids in her life. She wouldn't be able to settle down. Not with Josh. Not with anyone. Not for perhaps a very long time.

A tear leaked down her cheek and she chewed her lip in frustration. She had no one to blame for her plight but herself. Josh and his family had done everything they could think of to help her. Her father would move mountains to help, too, if he could. It was her own doing that she'd fallen in lust with Ramzi and married him without considering all the ramifications of a marriage with someone from such a different culture. Even after they'd married, she should've paid attention to her inklings about his true nature. Long before Jimmy was even conceived.

Now she and her son would pay for her mistakes for the rest of their lives.

Josh stirred in his sleep and groaned. He seemed uncomfortable. She took the pillow from the small of her back and slid it behind his head.

Without a flash of inspiration, without so much as a drumroll, Clare suddenly knew that she loved Josh Ryan. Loved him with a passion so strong and true it could never die. A different sort of emotion from whatever she had felt for Ramzi or for anyone before him. She had never been so sure of herself.

Her son was her life, of course, and always would be. And because of him, she would be forced to hide the two of them from Ramzi, who could destroy their relationship and their lives with a wave of his hand. But now someone else meant as much to her as Jimmy. And she would never put Josh in the position of having to defend her with his life again. She couldn't.

When she and Jimmy were prepared to leave, they would go without tears. Without looking back.

She would find a way to make their parting as easy on Josh as she could. At the very least he deserved to be free of guilt about her and Jimmy. He deserved…everything. But she had nothing to give him but safety and goodbye.

Josh stirred in his sleep. Knowing he was dreaming, he still couldn't force himself to wake. For some reason, he felt compelled into this dreamland. Compelled and eager to see it through. And so, he let his mind drop back into the murky world of light and shadow and let the images come.

"Hijo, *sit still and listen to Abuela Lupe. This is an important lesson.*" *He couldn't see his mother, but that was definitely her voice. If he lived a thousand years, he would never forget his own mother's soft, rich tones.*

But as much as he loved her and wished to make her happy, he couldn't do as she asked. His body jerked and strained with the desire to run. Needing the sunshine like he needed to breathe, Josh wanted to be back outside on his mare. Besides, this witch-craft stuff was stupid. He didn't care if Ethan and Maggie said they had fun with the potions and curses. The other boys teased him about it, and he wanted no part of such a weird game.

"Aw, Mama. Why do I need this stuff?"

Abuela Lupe touched his cheek to capture his attention. "I speak to you now in your dream, nieto. *You must have this lesson in order to become a savior."*

Was she nuts? "How can you talk in a dream, Abuela?" This felt too real. It couldn't be a dream, could it?

"You are special, mi hijo. *You have a power within you that your brother and sister do not share. But you must be open and practice. Use it. Do not turn your back on your talents."*

"What power?" He looked around, trying to decide if this might be a joke, some trick his little brother was playing at his expense.

His grandmother tsked at him. "Remember my words. Let your mind be free. When you see the light, go after it in your visions. Do not let the light escape your grasp, for that is where you will find your answers."

"Uh...visions?" Now that was over-the-top. If this wasn't a joke, it had just become too uncomfortable and embarrassing.

"You called me for help, Jose Joshua Ryan. Do not scoff or give up without trying."

He had called her? "How? How did I call you?"

"In your mind. You have the power to ask for what you want the most. The answers will come if you will allow the visions and do not hide from them."

Anger shot through his veins, sharp, hot and furious. "I don't want your damned visions. I hate being special. Take it away. Go away!"

His eyesight grew cloudy. Where there had been light and his grandmother's face, there now was nothing but mist.

Suddenly Josh felt his mother's hug, real and tender and safe, but invisible in the fog. Yet she wasn't there. She couldn't be there.

"Use it, mi querido," he heard her say. "Let the visions of light work for you. You still have the power."

Josh jerked awake with a killer headache.

"You okay?" Clare asked. "The captain announced we're ready to land in San Antonio. Another fifteen minutes and we should be on the ground."

Josh groaned and stretched. "We're going shopping when we land."

"Shopping?" Clare stared at him as if he were a talking horse. "Are you really awake?"

"Yeah, I'm wide-awake. And we're going to buy all new clothes in San Antonio—right after we find some aspirin."

They took a cab to the Riverwalk area because Josh insisted they not touch his pickup just yet. Clare trusted him without hesitation. She would do whatever he asked of her. But he had been acting freaky and sort of spacey ever since he'd had that nap on the last leg of their flight.

They wandered down the sidewalks along the banks of the slow-moving San Antonio River, under tall ebonies, live oaks and pecans until they found a boutique with Texas apparel. Josh insisted they buy every stitch of clothing brand-new. Even underwear.

"Get the salesclerk to remove the tags and we'll wear the new things," he told her when she'd picked out a pair of jeans and a T-shirt.

"Okay, but what'll we do with our old clothes?"

"Gather them up. We're going to toss them on the back of a moving van headed for Phoenix that I saw outside."

"What? You're crazy. I only bought this suit yesterday."

Josh turned a firm look in her direction. "I'll explain later."

Clare did as he had asked, but she was becoming worried about Josh. He'd been through a lot in the last couple of days. She couldn't wait until they got back to Zavala Springs. There, Maggie would help him. In the meantime, Clare could only humor him the best way she knew how.

While they were walking together past a multistory outdoor mall right above the river, Josh suddenly stumbled. He blinked and snapped his hand to his forehead.

"Josh?"

"The light. It's the light. But it's too damn bright." He staggered back and she reached out to steady him.

"Do you need a doctor?"

Josh jerked straight up and tore his arm from her grip. Turning his lips down in a scowl, he glared at her.

"Your purse." Ripping the shoulder bag right off her arm, he upended it and dumped the contents out on the sidewalk.

"Josh, for heaven's sake! What are you doing?" Squatting down before him, she gathered in wallet, lip balm and tissues as they floated to the ground. All the things, both great and small, came flying out. She grabbed every one as he pitched them, and made sure none of her belongings were lost or scattered.

He was muttering to himself and turning her shoulder bag inside out. "It has to be here," he said through a low growl. "I know it. It has…" His words drifted off as he plucked something shiny from the bottom of her bag.

"There." He held out a thumbnail-size metal thingy for her to see and dropped her bag. "A GPS chip. They've known where we were all along, just by following your purse. Damn it all to hell!"

It took a moment for the truth of what he'd said to register. *Someone had physically planted a bug on her!*

"Now…what do we do?" she asked.

Josh reared his arm back and pitched the chip into the San Antonio River. "Now we go home and get on with plan B. Your ex just messed with the wrong guy."

Chapter 13

Lucille's wheels made the trip between San Antonio and Zavala Springs in a record one hour and fifteen minutes. The two humans in her cab barely spoke a word the whole time.

As Josh pulled into town, he could sense Clare's tension. He knew the separation from her child for so long, and the fact her trip had not been what she'd expected, had taken a toll. She'd been counting on the United States government to put her life back together. Instead, it might turn into a nightmare.

Their throwaway cell was out of minutes and Josh hadn't wanted to stop to call Maggie. At well past supper time, he wondered if Jimmy would still be awake so Clare would get a chance to hold him. The boy's mama had been through a rough twelve hours. She'd been in the line of fire, saw a man shot and was told she might have to return her son to his father or be jailed as a kidnapper. *Then* she discovered she'd been bugged and the bad guys had probably tailed her all the way to Texas.

What he wouldn't give to be able to lift some of those worries off her shoulders. Not much he could do for her but deliver her safely, though. The best thing for her right now would be to have her son back in her arms.

Josh had expected the house to be quiet. Instead, when he'd turned down the street, he discovered the cheery sight of lights blazing full blast.

"Do you think something is wrong?" Clare sat all the way forward in her seat, placed her palms down on the dashboard and stared out the windshield at the brilliant yellow glow.

"Nah. We'd know if anything had happened."

"How would we know?" Clare's tired voice sounded scratchy and as tense as her shoulders.

Could he tell her the truth that he could barely stand himself? That both he and Maggie were witches and they had extra senses about each other? If Maggie had been in trouble, he would've known it without question.

Josh figured he would tell Clare all about it someday, certainly before they split apart for good. Just not today.

"Don't go begging for trouble where none exists," he said to calm her. "You have plenty of problems already. Twenty more seconds and we'll be inside and you can see for yourself that everything is fine."

He had hardly brought the pickup to a stop when Clare ripped open the door and dashed toward the house. She flew up the porch steps, ripped the front door open and entered. By the time Josh parked and made it inside, he could hear Clare's voice talking softly in some unseen part of the house.

When he walked into the kitchen, the first thing he saw was Clare sitting at the kitchen table with Jimmy wrapped in her arms. Her eyes grew shiny with unshed tears. She sat rocking and clasping her son to her chest as though she hadn't seen him in months instead of a little over one day.

Singing. That's what he'd heard. Clare wasn't talking, but crooning some soft lullaby to her baby as Maggie stood by the kitchen sink, dabbing at her eyes with a dishtowel. His heart pinged as he found his own eyes growing glassy with wetness.

Jimmy reared his head back and looked up at Clare. "Mommy!" The baby patted her cheek and giggled.

Clare groaned and Josh worried that she would break down into a sobbing, quivering disaster. Without considering the ramifications, he swung an arm around them both, intending to give her the support to get herself together.

The baby shrieked with laughter when he saw who held them. "Dada. Dada. Horsey!" Clapping and babbling, Jimmy bounced up and down.

Josh dared a glance at Clare. She used one hand to swipe at her cheeks but her face still held a smile. Lordy mercy, but she was the most beautiful woman he had ever beheld. Tough and resilient. Soft and sentimental when it counted. And sexy as hell all the time.

It took the three of them a good two hours to calm Jimmy down and put him to bed. By that time, Josh figured Clare would be ready to collapse. It had been one long, tough day after one long and terrific but physically demanding night. Neither of them had gotten more than a catnap in the last thirty-eight hours.

But Clare must have gotten a quick adrenaline rush, because she told Maggie she wanted to hear about Plan B now. Not to put it off till the morning.

Maggie turned on the pot of coffee and pulled a pan of brownies out of the oven where she'd been keeping them warm. When they all sat down around the table, Maggie looked into the exhausted faces of her brother and the woman she had already come to care about like a sister, and wished to hell she had good news to give them.

She'd dreaded having this conversation. After spending all day gathering information and researching every possibility, she had found there was only one way for Clare to get what she needed. Maggie surely wouldn't have wanted to have to face the stark reality of this plan had she been in the same position.

Wondering if Clare was as tough as she seemed, Maggie decided not to sugarcoat anything. "The only sure way for you to keep your son will mean stepping outside your old life, maybe for good. You might also need to occasionally step outside the law. Are you willing to consider it?"

"What's my choice? The law hasn't been able to help me, in fact, it's hindering me. If becoming an outlaw is what I have to do in order to keep my baby, then so be it." Clare took a deep breath and folded her hands firmly on the table. "Tell me."

Maggie would have given anything to be able to impart some hope. But she only had the truth to give. She checked out Josh's expression and found him sober and cold, but silent. This would be hard for him, too, she knew.

"You and Jimmy must start new lives," Maggie told her and then waited for the information to sink in. "The old Clare and Jimmy Chandler will need to disappear for good. You're to make a list of all the places in the world you have ever visited or ever had any friends, and then move to someplace else. You may never again contact any of your friends or acquaintances, and your relatives should consider you dead."

Clare gasped under her breath but keep her eyes trained on Maggie. "That's bad. The worst. What else do we have to do?"

"I've talked to Ethan about this," Maggie continued, "and he says you shouldn't even consider staying in Zavala Springs. There's an outside chance your ex could trace you here, and you really have to go to a place where you are totally unknown."

Clare shot a look at Josh, then firmly set her chin. Maggie was impressed with how well her new friend was taking it all in.

"There's more to disappearing than just a new name and a new address," Maggie continued more softly. "Stuff that has to do with never putting your real mailing address on anything, never taking a job in any industry where you've worked or trained and never taking up any hobbies that you might've had in the past. Never."

Clare opened her mouth, then quickly shut it again. Maggie couldn't imagine how hard this must be to hear.

"There's more," Maggie said with a sigh. "A lot more. In fact, it'll take us about a week to get you all set for your disappearing act. Are you sure you're willing?"

Clare hesitated and then said, "I'm a journalist. I prefer to expose lies rather than tell them. It's not in my nature." She glanced at the ceiling, up to the bedroom where her son lay sleeping. "But this isn't just about me. And I will do anything for Jimmy."

She stood and pushed back her chair. "I think we all need some sleep. Tomorrow we'll begin the lessons I'll need in order to learn how to disappear.

"I can't tell you how much I appreciate y'all changing your whole lives and routines for me. I don't know if I will ever be able to repay you. But just believe that you've saved a mother and her child and are appreciated." With that, Clare left the kitchen, heading upstairs to her sleeping son.

Maggie turned to her older brother. "Are you going to let them go off on their own?"

Josh stood up from the table and carefully shoved in his chair. "Don't see that I have much choice."

"But—"

"Look, sissy," he interrupted. "The lady wants a big family. Maybe if she goes off alone with Jimmy and starts a new life, she'll be able to find a guy who can give that to her."

Her brother fisted his hands, and Maggie guessed he was fighting the images of Clare with another man. Happy. Having children.

Josh spun around and headed for his room. "Go to bed, Maggie," he said over his shoulder. "Our generation of the Ryans aren't meant to have decent relationships. Just settle yourself to those facts and go on with your life. That's what I intend to do."

Ramzi's world had begun to shatter. He had boarded his private jet bound for Texas, but had been on the tarmac awaiting further directions from his private investigator. The incompetent fool had just given him bad news.

The more Ramzi thought of that damned woman stealing his only son, the more he felt like killing her for her treachery. His father had called a little while ago, saying he was preparing for his trip and eager to see his grandson again. Now time had turned against Ramzi, too.

"So, you admit you lost contact with her in San Antonio." He spit the words into the cell phone at his ear, and wished the investigator was standing before him.

"Yes, Excellency," the man replied shakily. "But we are not at a complete loss. One of our men has tracked their rental car back to the man who was with her. The trail leads to a rural area in south Texas. I have men on the way there."

"I shall join you in Texas within a few hours. If you get a lead on her whereabouts before I arrive, you are not to confront her. Is that understood?"

The hired man assured Ramzi that all precautions for safety had been taken this time. Then he arranged to meet Ramzi's plane and hung up.

Ramzi absently fingered the fluted dagger he had sheathed under his jacket at his waist. He'd had enough of Clare Chandler's tricks to last him an entire lifetime. She could not simply be allowed to steal from him and get away with it. Not if he was going to face himself in the mirror. And especially not if he had to face his father.

The next twenty-four hours dragged by for Clare. She knew she should be paying closer attention to Maggie's instructions and working harder at learning how to disappear, but she couldn't stop thinking of having to walk away from Josh.

She knew it was the right thing to do. Leaving him behind was the only way to be sure he'd be safe. Thoughts of him in D.C., standing there beside the car and facing that man with a machine gun, continued to haunt her day and night.

But being around him every day with her mind secretly made up to leave him also made her feel restless—unfinished. As though somehow the two of them had been designed to fit together, and her pushing away from him would be against the laws of nature.

He made her feel so good. He fed her needs, both emotional and physical. He'd kept her safe…and…he behaved almost as if he really loved her.

How could she leave all that behind? Tsking at such foolishness, she chided herself for being selfish. Her comfort and happiness certainly weren't good enough reasons to ruin a man's life. They were just neediness on her part.

"Clare? What do you think?" Maggie was speaking to her and dragged her back from the reverie.

"Oh, sorry. I guess my mind was someplace else." Yeah, like in bed making love to Josh—and it was only seven-thirty in the morning, for heaven's sake. "What were you asking?"

"I was just wondering—"

A knock on the kitchen door interrupted Maggie. At the same time, Josh strolled in from the other direction carrying Jimmy on his shoulders.

"I'll get it," Maggie said as she stood up to open the door.

Josh handed the baby over and Clare set him on his feet on the floor. Jimmy turned when he heard the voices at the back door and took off at a run. "La La! La La!"

"Como está, niño, mi querido!" Larado from next door entered the room carrying a cloth bundle in her arms.

Lara and Jimmy had spent time together when the baby had stayed over at her day care. Clare liked Lara a lot and apparently her son did, too. Rail-thin, with deep, expressive ebony eyes and raven hair, Larado Hinojosa had been widowed at the tender age of twenty-eight when her husband was killed on the last day of his third tour of duty in Iraq. Now she ran the only day care center in the county.

Jimmy clung to Lara's knees and begged to be picked up, but Lara's arms were already full.

She laughed, turned and offered the bundle to Clare. "Here," she said in her perfectly pronounced English. "You hold the baby a second while I say hi to our big guy."

Clare ended up with an armload of blankets, all wrapped around a baby she would have judged to be about two months old. "Wow, Lara," she said in amazement. "Where'd this itty-bitty one come from?"

Lara held Jimmy in her arms and brought him closer, pointing toward the sleeping child in Clare's arms. "See the baby, Jimmy? She's our newest friend."

Jimmy's eyes widened as he leaned over to get a better look. "Baby." He looked up at his mother as if to say, "Do we get to keep her?"

Lara jiggled Jimmy in her arms to keep him happy and spoke to the adults in the room. "I've suddenly become a foster mother. Totally unplanned. This poor little girl's parents were killed last night on that bad stretch of highway leading off the Delgado to the southwest. The baby was in the car, too, but buckled into her baby carrier in the backseat. Not a scratch on her, but now her mom and dad are gone and the sheriff can't locate any other relatives."

Josh stepped over to study the little girl. "Were they people from around here? Or were they visiting someone in Zavala Springs?"

Lara shook her head. "Apparently not. They were in a rental

car. Out of Houston. The agency there had a Virginia address for them, and our sheriff has calls in to their local law enforcement."

"What on earth were they doing on the Delgado heading south?" Maggie moved in close to the baby and stroked the little one's cheek.

Lara shrugged. "It seemed like they were driving toward Mexico. But going that way means taking the long way and crossing at the toll bridge at Roma north of McAllen." She turned to Clare. "That's in the middle of nowhere. And not much of a reason for strangers to cross there.

"Anyway," Lara added. "I came to ask if you could take care of the baby today for a while. Just until my daughter gets home from kindergarten at noon. I have a full house coming this morning. Six kids. My Jenna can help when she gets home. She's real good with the ones that are almost school-age and helps me make their lunches. But until then…" She looked exasperated. "I can make better arrangements for tomorrow if the baby stays that long. But can you help me out today?"

Both Clare and Maggie answered at the same time. "Sure!"

"No problem," Maggie said with a laugh and took a small duffel bag from Lara's shoulder.

Clare placed a soft kiss on the baby's forehead and sighed. "We'd love to help out, wouldn't we, Jimmy?"

Jimmy's forehead wrinkled in a frown as he reached for Josh. "No baby," he said and kicked his feet.

Josh pulled him from Lara's arms. "Come on, big guy. Let's you and I make ourselves some breakfast. Babies are women's work. We've got man stuff like banging on pans to take care of."

Clare's heart stuttered. She was feeling vulnerable enough with this sweet, sleeping baby in her arms. But as usual, just when she'd needed him, Josh had stepped in and made her wish things could stay this way forever. He seemed to be there during every emergency, whenever she needed a friend, and always when someone had to step in for Jimmy. He'd been doing that since the very first instant she'd ever laid eyes on him.

She could count on two hands the number of days left to be with him. Then she would never see him again. Why did he have to be so flipping perfect? Darn him.

Later that afternoon Josh came downstairs looking for Maggie. The house had become unusually quiet since Lara had retrieved the baby. Clare had put Jimmy down for his nap, and then stayed in the bedroom with him to get some rest herself.

On a mission, Josh felt changed. He'd been coming to this fork in his life's road for a few days now. But when he'd heard that story Lara had told about the baby and her parents, he'd made up his mind.

The thought of a fatal accident with no way to reach any relatives had driven a stake into his heart. What if that had been Clare and Jimmy, after they'd done their disappearing act? There would be no one listed as an emergency contact. No friends or relatives for the sheriff to find. No one would be available to take care of Jimmy or see to Clare.

It gave him the chills just imagining such a tragedy. He couldn't let them just go off into the world like that without a safety net.

"Maggie?" He poked his head into the P.I. office and found her working on the computer. "What's up?"

She didn't turn away from the screen but talked to him over her shoulder. "I've been checking the Internet looking for a lead to finding relatives for that baby Lara's taken in. I'm not having much luck, though."

"Let the sheriff do it. He has more clout with the authorities in other states than you do."

Maggie screwed up her mouth and turned her head to give him a look. "Our sheriff doesn't have near enough electronic knowledge or the time to learn. The baby's parents came from Alexandria, Virginia, and the authorities there put him in touch with some neighbors, but no one knows of any family. No one even knows why they were headed for Mexico. The sheriff has asked me to look into the possibility of relatives in other states. If they're out there, I should be able to find them eventually."

"Would you be able to find them if the baby's parents had *wanted* to disappear? Or if the government had planned for them to disappear—like in one of those witness protection programs?"

Maggie finally turned all the way around and looked up at him. "You're worried about something like this happening to Clare and Jimmy after they go away." It wasn't a question; she knew her brother too well.

Josh nodded.

"Well, then, why don't you go with them? It's not like you have a job or kids here that would compel you to stay."

He turned and started pacing the room. "I can't. She doesn't want me. I'm not the *guy*. If I did go, sooner or later I would be nothing but a lead weight around her neck. I can't do that to her.

"But I also couldn't stand not knowing if they're alive and well," he added as he swiped a hand across his face. "It would drive me crazy. I want to do everything in my power to make sure they stay safe, and to know immediately if they aren't."

Josh moved to his sister's side. "Help me, Mags. I've forgotten how…"

"To work the magic?" she asked with a grin. "I have a better idea. If you're really ready to take back the power, why don't you go ask Abuela Lupe for help? She's better able to teach you than I am."

"In Mexico? But… What if she won't see me? She wasn't too pleased with me the last time I saw her."

Maggie stood and tenderly put her hand on his arm. "She's your grandmother. She loves you. Go apologize for going along with our father and tell her you need help.

"Just try to stay out of *her* mother's way," Maggie added as she shivered involuntarily. "Great-grandmother or not, that's one old witch whose path you do not want to cross."

Chapter 14

It had been ten long years since Josh had last visited Mexico, but he hadn't forgotten a minute of the way to his grandmother's home. After an eighteen-hour drive from Zavala Springs through some rough territory, he entered a region of southern Veracruz state that looked fertile and lush. Josh always thought of the weather in south Texas as intense, but the acute heat and humidity here beat anything in the States.

A verdant land with melons, papaya and tobacco farms, this area of Mexico was known for its grand *estancias,* the huge tropical ranches that grew fat cattle along their rain-forest-laden riverbanks. He could smell the mango and pineapple from the road. Could even feel the earth and its magic, damp and thick in the air.

Bruja country. Witch country.

Stopping at the gate to his maternal family's *estancia,* he asked to visit his grandmother and handed over the expected payment to the gatekeeper. As he passed the guardhouse, Josh thought about Mexican folklore. Mexicans raised their children to know about witches and evil eyes and ghosts high in the mountains. In every market throughout the country, at least one stall would be selling scented candles, mysterious oils and herbs and boxes of powders that promised good luck, protection or success. Here in the tropical paradise area of Mexico, witchcraft ran rampant. This location, with its cool mountains and deep, shadowy forests alive in myth and legend, was the capital, the power seat, of Mexican witchcraft.

It gave him the creeps. But he swallowed back his nerves and continued down a narrow lane with a canopy of hundred-foot trees towering above him. Abuela Lupe would see him, he felt sure. Maggie had said she knew their grandmother still lived and was well, and that she would be happy to speak to her oldest grandson. He sure hoped so. But also he prayed that Lupe's mother, Maria Elena Ixtepan, who had to be over ninety by now, would not be anywhere around.

Driving through one of the small villages on the *estancia,* Josh looked out his window at pastel-colored houses without glass in their windows, at children splashing in the mud by the town well and finally at the tables and tents set up along the square where vendors sold everything from produce to statues of the saints. Market day.

He stopped, bought an iced bottle of soda pop and asked about his grandmother.

"*Sí. Sí.*" The man behind the tables filled with corn tortillas for sale grinned widely as he spoke to Josh in Spanish. "The good witch. The *curandera!* She lives in the big house. Up by the lake. You go. You will find her there."

Josh considered asking after his great-grandmother, too, but thought better of it. The last time he'd seen the wicked old woman she had been living in a shack on the side of a nearby mountain. Dealing in dark magic, the black side of Mexican witchcraft, Maria Elena spun her spells and cast her hexes from a thatched roof hut in the shack's backyard, under the watchful eye of a giant wooden red devil.

Grateful not to have to go back there, Josh followed the tortilla vendor's directions to find his grandmother. He pulled up in front of a nice, fairly modern one-story home at the side of a large blue lake. Nearly a dozen slender rowboats, painted in bright primary colors, sat stacked up in the water lilies next to well-kept docks, looking ready for a fishing expedition.

Surprised to see wires strung from wooden poles over to the house and stunned to hear the whir of electric motors coming from the place, Josh had to smile at how modern it seemed. He felt a little happier and less guilty thinking of his grandmother living in this nice place. It might not be the home she'd shared with her husband back on the Delgado, but it looked every bit as comfortable and pleasant.

Picking up the bouquet of roses he'd purchased at one of the town's stalls, Josh started up a concrete walkway lined with daisies. Before he took ten steps, his grandmother appeared on the front porch. As beautiful and vibrant-looking as he remembered, she stood there just staring at him with her warm brown eyes. Besides the shock of silver that had appeared in her shiny ebony hair, she hadn't changed a bit.

He hesitated as Abuela Lupe looked him up and down, then her eyes filled with tears as she opened her arms and beckoned him to come closer. It didn't take him two steps to walk into her arms for a hug. His own eyes filled as she whispered his name and how grateful she was to see him. Suddenly all his guilt landed back in his gut with a dull thud. He should've come to check on her long before now.

"Abuela Lupe, I…" His words shut down, choked off by the terribly dry lump in his throat.

"I love you, Josh. What happened in the past should stay in the past for us," she said with a beam. "Are those flowers for me?"

Lupe took the flowers and led the way into her living room. "I've prepared something for you to eat. I know you have come a long way. Everything is almost ready. Meanwhile have a glass of tea."

Josh followed her into the kitchen, but he couldn't help but think something wasn't right. "Uh, Abuela, how did you know to make food for me? How did you know I would be coming?" He expected her to make a comment about seeing him in one of her crystals or having a vision of his trip in one of her dreams.

Instead she smiled and said, "Your sister e-mailed me last night and told me you were coming."

"E-mail? You have a computer?"

She poured his tea and opened a small freezer and pulled out a couple of ice cubes. "Don't worry about the ice, it's from bottled water. And of course I have a computer. It's in my office."

Sitting down at her kitchen table, Josh scrubbed his hands across his face. "Abuela, I'm so sorry about what happened between you and my father. And I feel terrible about not visiting you before now. I'd like to make it up to—"

She waved away his words. "We don't have time for regrets. You've come for help. For lessons. First you'll eat and then we will begin."

"Did Maggie spill everything?" He was irritated with his sister for not telling him she'd been in contact with their grandmother by computer.

"No. No. I saw your pretty friend and her little son in a dream. I know you want to help them, and I'm proud of you, *nieto*. You've grown to be a generous and bighearted man. Your mama would be proud of you, too. She would say that you have earned respect. To her, that was the most important thing."

Josh swallowed the newly reformed lump in his throat along with half a glass of tea. He didn't deserve anyone's respect, least of all his dead mother's. Just take a look at what he'd done. He'd gone along as his father took Abuela Lupe back to Mexico and hadn't even tried to stop him. And then he'd been too busy feeling sorry for himself for nearly fifteen long years to check on his own grandmother. Add to that the problem of taking advantage of Clare when she'd been the most vulnerable, and he wasn't too proud of himself right about now.

But he was here on a mission, and needed to remember that. He vowed to be a better a man.

"So what's bothering you the most?" Maggie asked as she turned from the computer screen.

Clare didn't want to tell her she'd been daydreaming about Josh and lost in the waves of wanting. The damned man had only been gone a little over twenty-four hours and already she felt bereft and weepy. Just what would she do for the rest of her life?

"I'm sorry, I wasn't paying attention." She forced a watery smile. "I understand how it will be out there in the world for Jimmy and me alone and I'm not afraid. But…a couple of things are sort of nagging at me."

"What are they? Maybe if we talk about them, we can find a way over, under or around them." Maggie took her hand. "Look, Clare, I've grown to love you like a best friend over the last week. I'll do anything to make it easier for you. And for Jimmy. We all will. Just talk to me."

Clare sighed, grateful she'd met these lovely people and desolate that she would be leaving them all behind. "We've talked about these things until we're both sick to death of going over them. I'm sorry, Mags, but I still don't know how I'm going to be able to make enough money to support my son when I can't use my journalism degree or contacts. I won't even be able to prove to people that I have a college degree at all. I know other single mothers find a way, but…"

"Money. Check. What else?" Maggie dropped her hand and turned back to type something into the computer.

Clare tilted her head and narrowed her eyes at the serious manner Maggie had suddenly taken. "Um. Well, this one is just silly. Because I know I'll have to take a job and leave Jimmy in day care. But how am I ever going to be able to trust anyone I don't know to care for my son?"

Maggie turned her head to give her a look. "You trusted me with Jimmy in a little over twenty-four hours. And Lara next door, too."

Clare's heart softened toward the dear young woman. "I knew you loved him within minutes, and you wouldn't have let Lara keep him if you hadn't trusted her completely. I might not be that lucky again."

Now Maggie's eyes glazed over and she set her mouth as if she was trying hard not to cry. For a few seconds, Clare could see emotions and ideas racing across her expression and in her eyes.

"I think I have an idea." She held up her hand as Clare opened her mouth to pepper her with questions. "Let me work on it a while. Then we'll talk.

"In the meantime," she added, "let's you and me take a little ride. There's someone I've been wanting to talk to and I think you should meet him."

They grabbed their purses and Clare insisted on checking on her baby before they went anywhere. Next door at Lara's house Jimmy was playing with the other kids and barely noticed his mother as she kissed the top of his head.

A few minutes later when they climbed into Maggie's SUV, Clare put a hand on her friend's arm before she started the motor. "Have you found any relatives for that poor little lost baby that Lara's taken in?"

"Not yet. But I'm still working on it." Maggie's face took on a determined look and Clare just knew she would somehow work a miracle for the orphaned girl.

After driving for about half an hour, they pulled the SUV up to a gigantic gate in a six-foot-high stuccoed wall. A sign made in wrought iron over the gate said The Delgado Ranch. The men at the gate waved Maggie through.

"Where are we going?" Clare asked belatedly. "I didn't think you ever came out here. Not since…"

"Yeah, you're right. The curse. That's what most people believe. But my Granddad and Grandma Ryan would've had my head if I hadn't maintained some kind of a relationship with my father after I moved to their house in town. Through all the things he'd done, he was still their son, and still my dad, too. Family meant everything to them.

"I still keep in touch with my other grandmother in Mexico, too." Maggie grinned. "I guess family is what I do best."

No, Clare thought, *loving* is what you do best.

Twenty minutes after they drove through the gate they were sitting on a terrace under pecan trees, drinking lemonade and eating homemade cookies. A uniformed maid had shown them in through beautiful carved-wood front doors, and then led them out to a partially covered courtyard. A little taken aback by western opulence, Clare thought it was rich-looking but not at all like the flash and gold-flecked garishness of Ramzi's parents' house in Abu Fujarah.

Instead, this was understated elegance done in a southwest theme. She'd been in a few mansions like this before. The houses of wealthy Texas oilmen. But this one was where Josh, Maggie and Ethan had grown up. Somehow, their down-to-earth attitudes and easygoing styles didn't quite match all this grandeur.

She judged the sprawling fortress had to be at least thirteen thousand square feet. As they'd walked through the house, she'd noticed a few formal rooms but the main living area was a great room with a massive stone peninsula bar, stretching out over the planked wood floors. Behind a kitchen that looked as if eight people could comfortably cook there, dramatic windows had brought her gaze out to the central courtyard. The furniture both in the great room and in the courtyard wasn't the kind of stuff you'd be worried about the kids ruining. It was good and solid. Wood and leather chairs and tables plus plenty of chandeliers and overhead pot lights made the vaulted rooms seem cozy. She'd marveled at the stuccoed interior walls in their golden color, the timber-beamed ceilings and the Mexican artwork and carvings on the walls.

Below their feet in the courtyard was a fortunes' worth of flagstone tile, leading out to manicured gardens. There a water feature and a sculpture set a striking scene. Wow. The place was way out of her league. Her father was well off, but nothing like this.

A tall man in a Stetson hat and jeans walked out through the French doors and Clare recognized him as the man she'd seen at the funeral. Up close he looked a lot more like Josh than she'd thought at first. Her heart skipped a little.

Maggie went to her father and he bent so she could kiss his cheek. "Meet Clare Chandler, Dad. She has a story I want you to hear."

Brody Ryan raised his eyebrows. "Seems to me this pretty gal should be all Josh's business." When he didn't get a reply from Maggie, Brody took off his hat. "Is there something you think I can do for her, little sissy?"

"Maybe, Dad. Hear her story. And then, just maybe."

In the darkest hours of the morning, Josh and his grandmother took a break from their lessons. "Are you sure you want to keep going, Abuela? You must be tired."

Lupe patted him on the cheek. "You are a good boy, *nieto.* But we must finish tonight. You should return today. You are needed." He'd explained the story of Clare and Jimmy and she must know how important it was for him to get back.

He'd learned a lot tonight, and much of what he'd found out

had little to do with magic. White witchcraft was his heritage, passed down to him by the ancestors. Turning his back on it had been the first step toward his destruction.

The second step had been turning his back on his beloved grandmother. "Abuela, why haven't you come home to the Delgado? Why don't you come with me today? I won't let my father run you out of your own house—never again. I'm sorry I let him the first time." Josh hung his head, not quite able to look Lupe in the eyes.

She lifted his chin with her fingers. "*Nieto*. You have kept the anger for too long in your heart. I was not forced into coming back home to Mexico all those years ago. Despite what you, your father and my mother seemed to think. I came because the anger and grief had grown too large in me. I needed to walk away from the daily reminders of your mother, my only child. I needed a spiritual cleansing, the *limpia*. I wanted to find peace."

Josh felt the invisible weight on his shoulders growing lighter. "So why don't you come back home now? My father won't have any say in the matter. The house has always belonged to you. We need you, Abuela. We...I...love you."

"I love you, too, *nieto*. All of you. But the house I remodeled with your grandfather on the Delgado is no longer my home." She smiled and took Josh's hand. "It belongs to you now. Our grandchildren were always the point of adding on to the original cabin your great-grandfather Delgado built with his own hands on *his* father's land-grant acres. It and the ranch were always meant for our children, grandchildren—and their children."

The ache came back into his chest. "But you know that won't happen now. Your mother punished us for going along with our father, and we deserved it. I can't tell you how sorry..." He couldn't finish.

Patting Josh's hand, she nodded her head. "I know. I have tried to reason with my mother. To make her understand that the punishment was too severe for you children when, if anyone deserved to be punished, it was your father. And it was much too extreme because I had *wanted* to come home."

She stopped nodding and sighed. "I will keep trying with my mother, but she is a stubborn woman who has let difficult circumstances turn her to the black way.

"You must not let that happen to you, *nieto*. Do not ever turn your back on the white magic. No matter what."

"*Sí*, Abuela. I'll remember what you taught me."

"Good." She turned to her crystals and potions. "In my dream I saw our old *casa* at the Delgado. You and the woman you strive to protect were living there with her son. All of you were playing outside in the sunshine. Once again there was the laughter of a child around the house."

Josh shook his head sadly. "Can't be true. I told you they have to go far, far away. No one is supposed to know where they are. It's too dangerous. That's why I need to be able to check on them with the magic. I won't harm them by telling anyone. But I've gotta know they're safe."

When his grandmother just gave him a wry smile, he went to her side and put his arms around her. "Please, Abuela. Come home."

This time she just laughed. "Joshua, how dear you are. But I cannot leave. I do not wish to go. I have my patients. I am the *curandera*. What would they do without me? They need me. And I have my husband. He needs me."

"What? You've remarried?" Josh was stunned. Why hadn't he known? Why hadn't he asked? Damn, it looked as if he really had turned into a self-obsessed bastard.

She raised her eyebrows and smirked at him. "You think a woman of seventy-two cannot be attractive enough to a man? When *you* reach that number of years, you will see that age does not diminish the lust between a man and a woman."

He raised his hands, palms out, to placate her. "I didn't say any such thing. And I don't think it. I was just surprised I didn't already know, that's all. Where is your husband tonight? Why haven't I met him?"

"My husband is on a cattle-buying trip. He manages the cattle operation here on the *estancia* for my father's family. For my cousins who now own the ranch. My life continues to be involved in the cattle business no matter where I live." Chuckling, Abuela stepped to a cabinet in order to retrieve red candles and continue the training. "There is much more for you to learn and very little time left, *nieto*. Stop asking questions and come back to work."

A few long, difficult hours later, Josh was packing up witchcraft supplies, getting ready to return home. "Thank you, Abuela. I appreciate everything you've done."

Lupe couldn't let him leave like this. "There is one more thing," she told him. "Much of the darkness surrounding you when you arrived is now gone. But I wish to remove the rest with a *limpia*, like I taught you to do. When you return to Texas it will be to live in the sun, not the shade."

He stood with a perplexed look on his face, and she wanted him to give her another hug. But not yet. He needed her to be strong for him. She could give him this much, and perhaps even more later.

When he had gone, she would go to visit her mother. This problem her grandson carried on his shoulders would not go away so easily, and Lupe wanted a cure, not a bandage.

"Come with me, *nieto*." She lead him through the house to the room with the altar. Earlier, she'd placed colorful flowers in amongst the pictures of the saints.

As they came closer to the altar, she felt warmth and lightness washing over her grandson's aura. She rubbed an egg over his arms, neck and head. Next she brushed a long bundle of dried leaves over his body while she whispered the proper incantation.

"Take this egg with you and throw it over the second bridge on the road," she instructed him. "All the bad spirits will flush away down the river with the egg." Praying for his protection and for the bad spirits to be removed from his body, she asked that luck be with him.

"Be strong and do what is called of you, *nieto*." She kissed him on the forehead. "Now, go in peace."

Chapter 15

Squirming in Lucille's passenger seat, Clare tried to catch glimpses of Josh's profile out of the corner of her eye as he drove them away from Maggie's place. He'd only been back in Texas for a little under twelve hours and had asked her to go for a ride. The very nearness of him in the pickup's cab left her panting and breathless. How foolish could she be? To want something so badly, even knowing that if he stayed close to her it might get him killed.

The idea of potentially endangering people made her feel a little like a Typhoid Mary, bringing death and destruction to all those around her. She was constantly looking over her shoulder, worrying that one of Ramzi's men would be right behind. But even today—the day before she and Jimmy would leave forever on the bus—Clare had never wanted any man more than she wanted Josh.

"Thanks for making time this afternoon to go with me," he told her without taking his eyes off the road. "I have something I'd like to show you…and something important I need to tell you."

Clare looked around and noticed the direction they'd been heading. "Where are we going? To the Delgado?"

He threw her an odd look. "Yeah. To one part of it. I want to show you the old Delgado homestead. It's where my ancestors first began the dream of this ranch."

"Your ancestors, were they the ones named Delgado?"

"Delgado was my mother's maiden name. She grew up here. Her father was one of a long line, dating back to the time when this part of Texas belonged to Mexico.

"My grandfather and grandmother had no sons," he continued, "so when my grandfather died, he left the land to his son-in-law, my father, according to the Mexican inheritance ways. But the old homestead and a few acres still belong to his wife, my Abuela Lupe."

Josh turned the pickup down a road Clare had never noticed before and headed off through wood-fenced fields where cattle were grazing. "Oh, look there in the distance. Horses. And it's mothers with their babies. How wonderful."

"Yeah, this is a fine time of year in south Texas." Josh took a deep breath. "Those mares make a pretty picture, don't they? Now I wish Jimmy was here. I think he would've loved to see this."

Clare heard the wistful tone in his voice, and knew Josh would miss her and her son as much as they were going to miss him. The tears she'd thought were swallowed down began threatening again.

Yes, her son would have loved seeing the baby horses with their mamas. But Clare had wanted these last few hours alone with the man she had grown to care about beyond words. She had to let him know what he meant to her. She needed to find a way to tell him, but to make him see that it was too dangerous for them to be together in the future.

In a few minutes they pulled up in the yard of a fascinating old two-story house surrounded by huge leafy trees. Not as immense or over-the-top opulent as Josh's father's house, this one looked like a home built just for family.

She stared through the windshield at the wraparound porch and at the various wood and colorful stucco sidings that each level of the house had been made from, and totally missed Josh getting out and coming around to open her door until he was there.

"Come on inside," he said as he helped her out of the pickup. "I'll turn on the electricity, open the windows and get the fans going. It's actually pretty comfortable in there even in the heat of the day. It won't take a moment."

He caught her arm, urging her up the porch stairs. Even through the cotton shirt, she could feel his touch like an electric shock. The house suddenly became much less interesting. All her attention was back on the man.

Josh insisted that they take a tour of the barns and the house once the place had aired out. He spoke to her of his family's history. Of the hard work and love that had gone into making the house a home.

Just as they came inside, thunder rolled from off in the distance. A late-afternoon storm was headed their way. But maybe they would be back at Maggie's before it hit.

Clare couldn't concentrate on either Josh's words or the upcoming weather. Whenever they stood this close together, her heartbeat picked up, her nipples tingled and her brain fogged over.

Josh pointed out the pretty chatskies his grandmother had left on nearly every shelf and counter. Candles, statues, quaint little bottles full of what looked like dried herbs. Then he took her into a small room that contained an altar, with pictures of saints above it. Clare had seen these kinds of things before in the houses of friends whose parents had been raised in Mexico.

"I...uh...wanted to talk to you," Josh began. He watched her in that intense way of his. "I didn't want you to leave before I could explain..."

"Explain what?" Clare could barely hear what he said past her own thudding heart. "You don't owe me an explanation. If anything, I owe you—the world. My life. My son's life. I can never repay you and your family for what you're doing for me."

He touched her cheek, watching her eyes with a dangerous, desperate look that almost scared her. Instantly she was moist with desire. Her whole body ached for him.

"Yeah, well," he began as he raked his fingers through his hair and turned away. "We live with a secret—Maggie, Ethan and I. There's another family heritage we carry besides this old place and the Delgado ranch. Our mother's family in Mexico is...what you would call *different*."

"Josh you really don't owe me any explanations."

"No, I need to say this," he blurted out as he turned back to face her. "I've thought for nearly all my life that I could run away from it. But now I don't want to live like that anymore. I want to say it aloud. I want you to know.

"My mother, her mother and her mother's mother," he said on a long sigh, "came from a line of witches."

At her intake of breath, Josh took her hands. Which made her stop breathing altogether.

"It's true, Clare. I swear it. I know it sounds nuts, believe me. But my brother, sister and I have inherited the same abilities as our grandmother. We've been taught to do the spells and hexes, and now I even know how to do a cleansing."

When he let go of her in order to pace the small room, Clare's heart started up again. He sounded so sincere, so sure of himself, and he only confirmed what Maggie had already told her. But this time, Clare's reaction was different. Josh Ryan meant everything to her. If he said he was a witch, she believed him.

He stopped pacing and faced her. "You're important to me. What you think is important. But you had to know the truth before you left forever.

"Are you laughing yet?" He added that last sentence so quietly, she almost missed it.

But she definitely caught the implication. He thought she might not believe and would smirk at the idea of him being a witch. But she wasn't laughing.

"No, Josh. I'm not scoffing at what you said. I believe everything you have ever told me."

This time the look he gave her was so intense it almost brought her to her knees. Her heart raced and she felt a flush of warmth running up her body to her cheeks.

"Then let me help you." He walked to the altar and lit a couple of the candles. "I want to do a cleansing for you. To rid your heart of any guilt you might have about taking Jimmy from Ramzi. You did what you had to do for your son, and I want you to be able to live with it.

"And then when you leave for good, I want you to take a protection charm with you," he continued. "Will you do those things for me?"

Oh Lord. She would do anything he asked. Anything but cause him harm. These requests of his should be easy.

"Of course. You're important to me, too, Josh. In fact, I—"

He took her by the shoulders. "Don't. Whatever you have to say. Just don't.

"Our time left together is short." He absently massaged her shoulders with his big hands. "Let's not say too much and ruin it. Okay?"

Clare nodded. Talking was overrated, anyway. But she could think of a couple of actions that would definitely be happening today. She wouldn't allow him to be in danger because of her, but she *could* show him what he had come to mean to her. There was plenty of time left for that.

And it might just be the best afternoon of her life. At least, if she had her way it would be.

With the thunder coming closer, she stood still as he rubbed an egg over her and whispered some words she didn't understand. The warmth in her core spread throughout her body until the glow burned brightly and her body flamed, almost painfully. Lightness and lightning crackled from his fingers to her skin and back again.

Finishing the cleansing by brushing herbs and leaves over her back and shoulders, Josh cracked the egg in a bowl and declared she was free of the bad spirits. She felt a special kind of ease come over her, but by then she was so sensitive to his touch her whole being hummed.

The rain began in earnest as he blew out the candles and turned his back to pack away his cleansing supplies. Clare could stand it no longer. She moved in behind him and put her arms around his chest as far as they would go.

"Say goodbye to me without words," she begged. "Let me tell you how I feel by my touch alone. I want to know the joy of having you inside me. One more time. Please."

Josh spun and pulled her tight. "It wouldn't be right. We shouldn't. You're leaving and it's for the best."

The rest of his objections were lost when he sighed deeply and nuzzled the side of her neck, mumbling words in Spanish that she couldn't understand. She could feel him surrounding her, felt the brush of his denim jeans against hers. The scent of his citrusy aftershave brought back the memory of their one night together and all her senses prickled.

A flash of lightning and the crash of thunder separated them for an instant. In a flash of his own, Josh picked her up and took the stairs three at a time. She heard a door open and then slam shut behind them, but all she could see, feel and hear was Josh as he held her tightly against his chest. He pulled her into his embrace as he lowered her back down.

One of his thighs moved between her legs and she felt his arousal. Immediately rigid. Powerful and demanding. Thrilling.

Lightning shivered between them as well as outside the windows as he took her mouth, setting off flashes of neon colors behind her eyelids. His wicked lips teased and seduced. When he moved to claim her neck, her head fell back.

Kissing down her throat to the tender spot at the base, Josh groaned and she moaned in return. Oh my, he made her feel so good. His hands found her breasts and he massaged them through her clothes.

Not enough. Not nearly enough.

Clare needed to be naked. Needed to feel his hands on her skin. She ripped the shirt off her shoulders and undid her bra. Then she started clawing at Josh's clothes. He chuckled at her impatience, but had his shirt and pants off before she blinked.

Filling his hands with her breasts, he bent and took one sensitive nipple into his mouth. His lips were hot, so very, very hot, as they suckled and nipped at her tender flesh.

She shook all over. Her legs felt rubbery. Her insides churned with heat and throbbed in a kind of exquisite pain.

Urgent. The need became more urgent as she ran her hands through his hair and became caught in a vortex, a lust-filled whirlwind of wants and needs.

After another endless, dizzying kiss, the two of them tore at their remaining clothes until they were naked and panting. Josh reached for her. Using one hand to drag her close and the other to skillfully stroke her, he ratcheted the tension to improbable heights.

"Now," she begged. She could hear the desperation in her voice, knew there was a bed somewhere behind them, but she couldn't wait another second.

As the winds picked up and crashes of thunder intruded on their intimacy, she threw her arms around his neck, jumping up to wrap her legs around his waist. Josh spun them as he helped lift her bottom and held her tight. He leaned her back against the door, kept his hard gaze locked with hers and plunged himself inside.

Surging upward, he filled her. As though driven by the same demons that had worked her into a frenzy, he slid out and back in again, lunging into her with a hot, hard joining. At the same time he plundered her mouth until she was left trembling and frenzied. Caught on the edge of release, Clare clung to him as tears leaked from her eyes and rolled down into their joined mouths.

Sensation swamped her before she was ready, battering her in a powerful climax. Josh picked up speed then, pounding, pounding, until her body tightened around him and she came again. One more deep thrust and he followed her over the edge.

Sobbing, she said his name over and over. When he straightened his shoulders enough to look her in the eyes, she saw the same tears on his cheeks that were on her own. He pressed a gentle kiss to her forehead and lowered her back to her feet.

"I didn't hurt you, did I?" His voice was rough, his words a raspy whisper.

"Not at all." She swiped at her eyes and reached for her strewn clothes. "I wanted us together that way today. I needed it— needed you. One last time."

He reached out to her, but she turned her back and slid into her jeans. She couldn't bear for him to touch her again. Not now. Not since she had already said her goodbyes in the only way she knew how.

They dressed in silence and headed down the stairs. The storm was almost over. The thunder and lightning had passed. All that was left were light raindrops, drizzling sadly on the range like the despondent tears inside her heart.

Josh couldn't believe he'd behaved so roughly with Clare. What had happened to his resolve and all his vows? There could never be enough time or the right words for him to tell her how he felt. But she'd given him an idea of what she felt toward him. Saying goodbye now was going to be harder than ever.

Because he knew her now. Knew her deepest desires and had figured out that what she needed the most was to be a mother totally unlike her own. Clare wanted a big family with a lot of babies for her to love in order to prove something to herself. Mainly that she was a better mother than hers had ever been. And that she was worthy of the mother's love she had never received.

She deserved a lot more than love. Josh knew, because he loved her beyond measure and it still wasn't enough. He would give her the world, but he couldn't give her those babies. Just loving her like he did would be so much less than she deserved.

When they reached the front porch, the rain had stopped. But both of them hesitated at the top of the steps. He knew he couldn't just drive away. Every minute was precious to him. But he couldn't touch her again, either.

Josh had picked up his Stetson when he'd locked the front door behind them. Now he stood on the porch, looking out at the range and fiddling with the hat in his hands. Clare's hands were in her pockets as she rocked back and forth and stared blankly into space.

There should be something they could say to each other. He ought to be able to come up with a goodbye that didn't sound arcane or idiotic. Perhaps the truth would work.

"I would go with you, but..." he began.

"I want you to go with us, but..." Clare said at exactly the same time.

She laughed, but the cheer didn't reach her eyes. "Goodbyes are hard. Jimmy and I will be okay, Josh. You don't need to worry about us. Maggie has everything all planned out and taken care of. This way is best."

He nodded, but couldn't speak. He couldn't even bear to look her in the eyes. She made him feel alive, and he hadn't been alive for years. Maybe not since before his mother died. What would life be like without her? *Unbearable*.

Finally, she broke the silence first. "Don't forget us."

Past the lump in his throat and around the deep ache in his chest, he managed, "Oh yeah, that'll happen. Like maybe I'll forget when flowers start growing in hell. Or when babies run marathons. Or maybe when politicians start telling the truth, that's when I'll forget you two."

She stared up at him as tears welled in her eyes. "Oh, Josh. I wish…"

Emotions strung tight, he felt desperate to tell her. Tell her exactly how much he had to give. But he couldn't. Just couldn't. He would give her and Jimmy his life in an instant. But he did not have what she wanted the most.

He couldn't bear listening to her sweet voice for another minute, nor standing this close and smelling her secret musky scent without pulling her into his arms. He took her elbow and marched them out to the pickup.

"Your bus leaves in a few hours," he said gruffly. "You and Jimmy need your rest. I'll take you back now."

That's what he'd said. But what he'd meant was, *I love you and my life is ending. I can't do this. I can't let you go.*

Instead of saying what he felt, instead of giving in and doing the wrong thing for her, he dug into his gut for courage, loaded her into Lucille and drove them back to town.

Ramzi's cell phone rang from somewhere he couldn't see in the dawn light of his motel room. He hadn't slept more than a few minutes in this crummy rural town, and the tension in his body and in his mind kept him wound as tight as a violin string. His nightmares had left him shaky and terrified.

He'd dreamed of losing—and of that horrible American woman he had mistakenly married being the winner. For those inadequacies, he had died a thousand agonizing deaths of pure humiliation.

But Ramzi would never let that happen in real life. Not if he had to kill her to stop it.

He finally located and answered the phone, still half-asleep but ready to spring into action. "What is she doing? Does she know she's being watched?"

The rental car had led them to Zavala Springs. Late last night, the P.I. had located the house where Clare had been staying with his son. His men spent the last few days asking all over the area for any new woman with a small child, and they'd finally come up with an old house on a side street in this tiny nowhere town.

Satisfied for the moment, Ramzi decided then that they couldn't just storm the house and take the baby. But he'd left a man watching the place and waited for an opportunity.

"The woman seems unconcerned about being observed, Excellency. But she and the child are on the move. Another woman has loaded their suitcases into an SUV and they're heading through town."

"Where is she going?" Ramzi screamed into the phone. "Do not lose her."

"Wait," his man suddenly interrupted. "It looks as if they are stopping at a bus station. Yes, they are. And now they seem to be unloading the suitcases in order to put them on a bus."

"Keep them in sight and stay on the phone with me. I will join you in a few minutes."

His chance. At last! That bloody woman was going to be sorry she had ever tried to cheat him.

Ramzi grabbed his clothes and stuck a newly purchased gun in his pocket. Today was the end of his quest. He swore to win this time. He would not live with the alternative.

Lost. Angry. Inconsolable.

Josh wandered around Maggie's house while the emotions poured through him. He grew angrier at the world with every step.

He hadn't gone with his sister when she'd taken Clare and Jimmy to the bus. There would've been no way of saying another goodbye.

But now he couldn't think straight. His mind seemed muddled. Where was he going to find the strength to go on?

Not enough time had gone by to check on Clare and Jimmy in his crystal. They'd hardly had enough time to board the bus yet. But he couldn't stand not knowing.

Heading to the walk-in closet Maggie had set up as an altar room, Josh shoved his hands in his pockets. But he immediately pulled his left hand back out again with his fingers clutched tightly around what he'd found. Clare's protection charm lay in the palm of his hand. He'd forgotten to give it to her before she left.

Without wasting a moment, Josh grabbed the keys to Lucille and took off. He had no idea where Clare and Jimmy were headed on the bus, but he had a feeling they would at least start by traveling to Mexico. Crossing over and back would muddy their escape route. Still, she needed the protection charm he'd made for her. It was the only way he could be sure the two of them were safe.

He made it to the bus stop just in time to see the bus heading south out of sight. Maggie stood in the middle of several people milling about, dabbing at her eyes with a tissue.

Josh stopped long enough to check. "Is their bus headed for the border?"

Maggie nodded. "Why? What's wrong?"

"Get in," he urged.

She did as he said and soon they were on the road leading to the border crossing. "She doesn't have the protection charm I made for her," he told his sister. "Do you think we can catch them before they cross into Mexico?"

"Sure. They have to walk across the border bridge in order to catch a Mexican bus on the other side. Jimmy will slow her down for sure.

"But you shouldn't worry about her, bubba. They're going to

live with Abuela Lupe. Only for a while. Maybe a year or so. They'll be safe there."

In a way Josh wished Maggie hadn't told him. Not that he would worry more. No. They would be safe with his grandmother for sure. But now that he knew, his plans to visit more often were on hold. It would be difficult for him to stay away. But he had to.

The two-lane highway leading to the border crossing seemed extra busy this morning and Josh couldn't catch up to the bus. By the time they arrived at the bus stop near the bridge, the bus was stopped and empty.

"We've missed them." The black cloud enveloped Josh's spirit again.

"Check your crystal. Maybe they've gotten stopped at the checkpoint."

Josh flipped out the seeing crystal his grandmother had given him and tried to find them. What he saw instead gave him a chill.

"Aw, hell. There's a long black Porsche coming up fast to the bridge. The only possible reason I'm seeing it in the crystal is that it's her ex. He's somehow found where they're headed and he's going to reach them before they cross over."

Josh jumped out of Lucille and took off toward the Rio Grande border bridge. It was maybe a hundred yards away from the bus stop, but from here he could see Clare and Jimmy slowly walking hand in hand, approaching the bridge.

Then he spotted it. The sleek black car bearing down on them. Picking up speed, the driver drove recklessly and appeared headed toward them in a way that would take the car right over them. *No!*

Running full out, Josh repeated the incantations he knew that might work in this situation. Not sure enough of his magical skills, he began calling Clare's name, praying she would hear him above the traffic noise.

Please, Clare. Hear me, he prayed. *Run for it!*

Clare didn't turn. Didn't seem to hear his shouts. But someone else far away was listening. Someone who knew exactly what to do.

As the Porsche reached impossible speeds and drew within twenty feet of Clare and the baby, she must have finally heard the car accelerating and turned. She grabbed Jimmy and jerked to the right, trying to avoid the impending collision.

The Porsche jerked right, too, in a move that seemed calculated to kill them both, but the driver never slowed. Within a few feet of them, the car went out of control, careened off the road and flew straight into the bridge abutment thirty feet down the embankment.

The noise was deafening. Instantly an explosion of fire and heat drove out all other sounds. The plume of black smoke that followed told the tale. Clare's ex-husband would no longer cause her any trouble.

Chapter 16

Josh sat in Maggie's kitchen ten days later, his elbows on the table and his head in his hands. *They'd been saved. Both Clare and her baby had been back here safe and sound.* And then the worst had happened.

They were gone, once again on the run and having to stay out of sight. This time, he and Lucille had had the dubious job of driving Clare and Jimmy to Abuela Lupe's house in Mexico—and out of his life for good.

"Are you still hanging around feeling sorry for yourself, bubba?" Maggie strolled into the kitchen and headed for the coffeepot.

"I can't seem to find anything useful I want to do, sis."

"Is that so?" Maggie sat down across from him and put the contents of a packet of sweetener into her mug.

"Why did things have to get so screwed up?" he asked with a whine in his voice he didn't much like. "It was all over. Her ex would never be able to threaten her again. She was free to do whatever she wanted. Go wherever made her happy. Then Ramzi's father had to step in and threaten jail once more if his grandson wasn't returned to Abu Fujarah.

"It's nuts," Josh complained. "The U.S. taking sides against their own for oil. It's not fair."

Maggie smiled at her big brother, but his head was lowered and he didn't see her do it. The poor guy was hurting, and she had been wanting to find some way of giving him a reason to live again. Now maybe she'd come up with just the thing. No one could cure his need for Clare and Jimmy, she knew. And nothing would ease his pain on their account. But she'd just had an idea that might take his mind off them occasionally.

"Josh." She said his name softly and put her hand over his on the table. "Can I talk to you about a couple of things?"

He looked up into her face with the curse of his pain etched into his expression. "Okay."

"I've been trying to locate a family member for the orphaned baby that Lara's keeping next door. You remember?"

Still looking miserable, he nodded silently.

"Well, I haven't had much luck and I've been thinking of taking the little girl in myself. Adopting her eventually if I still can't find any relatives and have to give up the search." Maggie looked down into her mug and waited for her brother to make a comment. As usual, she couldn't keep quiet. "I mean, I work at home for the most part and Lara's right next door if I need help. What do you think of me adopting a child?"

"I think it's a terrific idea to take her in, Mags. I'm all for it. But I wonder if our family's curse won't stop an actual adoption from taking place. I'd given some thought to adopting myself, uh, back before Jimmy left. But I'm just not sure how the curse works."

Maggie chuckled. "Me, neither. But I choose to believe it has to do with having babies of our own. Babies whose blood would be linked to our father. Maybe adoption wouldn't count.

"And maybe I'm willing to try it anyway." Maggie watched her brother's reactions carefully. He seemed to have momentarily forgotten his troubles as she had hoped.

"And while I've been looking to find any of the baby's relatives, I've discovered there are many, many lost children. And lots more kids out there who are in need of someone's help." This was it, and she hoped he would take the bait. "I can't stand the idea of no one being there to help those little ones. So I've decided to change the focus of Granddad Ryan's P.I. business. I want to concentrate the investigative side of the business on babies and children of all ages. And then I want to try going into the business of bodyguarding children, as well."

"Bodyguarding? Why would children need a bodyguard?"

"Well, it seems to me that Jimmy could've used a bodyguard more than a few times." She let that sink in and then hurried on. "And I know of a couple of Granddad's old clients who might have a need for that kind of service now and then. I'm sort of hoping Ethan will want to join the business when he's done with the Secret Service. He knows all about bodyguarding and could really help us."

"Us?" It was a question, but his eyes said he knew exactly where she was leading.

"Yeah, I was hoping you might be willing to join the business, too. After all, if I'm going to have a baby in the house, I'll need you and Ethan to do the actual legwork for the business that I can't accomplish on the computer."

She hoped she'd said enough to catch his interest. "What do you say?"

Josh rubbed at his jaw. "There'd be a lot I'd have to learn."

Got him.

"Yes, but you've already learned so much by helping Clare and Jimmy, and Ethan and I can teach you the rest.

"Come on, Josh, say yes."

"Maybe." He sat straight up in his chair. "Let's develop a business plan first. You like plans well enough. Do one for this bodyguarding thing. Then I'll consider it."

A few weeks later Josh had just finished talking to Ethan about the new business plan. His brother was packing up his things in D.C. and was nearly ready to leave on his way home to Zavala Springs. Maggie had gotten the sheriff's permission to move the orphaned baby girl over to her house. Things were swinging along on the bodyguarding business. This old house that used to belong to Grandpa Ryan was about to get very crowded.

It made Josh think of Clare and Jimmy in Mexico, staying in that cozy house with his grandmother and her husband. He supposed he thought about Clare and Jimmy nearly all the time. But this particular thought concerned their comfort. He wondered if they needed anything.

His crystal could only tell him if they were in trouble, and it had been clear since they'd been gone. But Josh felt he needed more information about their welfare.

He had the idea that Maggie kept in touch, if not with Clare directly, then with Abuela Lupe. So he got up and went looking for his sister to ask how they were doing.

Before he got to the kitchen door, Maggie came in carrying the baby in her arms. "There you are," she said. "I've been looking for you."

"I was just coming to find you, too." Josh got a little distracted by the beautiful little girl. "What are you calling her?" he asked with a nod to the baby.

"Her name, of course. Emma Sheldon is what her parents put on her birth certificate."

"Pretty. But Emma Ryan would be nice, too." Josh looked up

from the child in his sister's arms and noticed Maggie staring at
him in a sad way.

"So what did you want?" Maggie asked abruptly.

"What? Oh. Uh…I was wondering about Clare and Jimmy.
I'm concerned that they aren't comfortable with Abuela Lupe and
her husband. That's a pretty small house…considering. And…"

"You haven't asked about them at all in the last few weeks,"
Maggie interjected. There was a skeptical look on her face, but
Josh also spotted a twinkle in her eyes. "I thought you'd decided
to just go on with your life."

Go on with his life? What life? He was barely getting by day
by day. Hour by hour. Minute by minute. Without them in his
life, the whole thing seemed meaningless. The only way he'd
gotten through at all was by helping Maggie with her business
plans for the children. He'd decided that if he couldn't have his
own kids, this business would be one thing he could do for all
the kids in need. But that still didn't get him through the long,
miserable nights.

He couldn't answer Maggie, not without sounding like the
fool he had become. So he just shook his head quietly.

"Josh, if you were Clare, what would you need the most?"
Baby Emma began to fuss quietly in Maggie's arms.

Not able to dwell too closely on Clare's needs, Josh came up
with the first thing that hit his mind. "Money. If she had lots of
money then she and Jimmy could live in their own house and she
wouldn't have to worry about working or anything."

Maggie chuckled as she jostled the three-month-old girl in her
arms. "Well, that may not be number one in Clare's mind at this
point, but it's a good idea. And where would you get hold of a
lot of money if you could send it to her?"

That question took a bit more thought. "Dad," Josh finally
answered. "I'd borrow it from Dad.

"Great idea, Mags." Eager to face his father right away, Josh swung around, grabbing his keys on the way out the door. "I'm on my way to the Delgado," he told Maggie over his shoulder.

"Josh, wait! There's something else I need to tell…"

Her words were lost to the south Texas winds as Josh ran to his pickup and started it up. Whatever else his sister had to say could wait until he returned.

For the first time in longer than Josh could remember, his father had something he needed. And Josh planned on making his father step up to the plate.

It was about time.

Abuela Lupe climbed the solitary path up the mountainside on the way to her mother's house. Traveling in the heat of the day, she carried her mama's medicines, and, just to please her, a treat of fresh mangoes.

Even at her advanced age, Maria Elena still practiced as the local *bruja*. But anyone who came to consult a black witch, seeking curses or hexes, came in the dark of night. Not in broad daylight. So Lupe always made her weekly visits to her mother in the middle of the day.

Today she had something special on her mind.

When her frail mother, accompanied by her live-in aide, greeted Lupe on the path to her front door, it was with a scowl on her face. Lupe's heart thumped. Would Maria Elena ever be able to let go of the black bitterness surrounding her heart? Lupe did not want her mother to die while such a shadow covered her soul.

Today she would try again to make her mother see the light.

"Mija." Maria Elena greeted her as usual. "I see you have come seeking another favor of the black witch."

"No, Mamacita." Lupe turned the mangoes and medicines over to the twenty-four-hour-a-day aide she'd hired long ago to care for her mother. "I have come to see how you are feeling and to spend time with my mother. That is all."

Maria Elena lifted her hand in a dismissive gesture. "I know better. The last time I granted your request for a curse you were not pleased with the results. Why should I work magic for you again?"

Lupe helped her mother to settle into her favorite stuffed chair on the open front porch of her tiny home. "I do not need magic from you today, Mama. And even that last time, all I had requested was a way to keep the bad man from finding the woman named Clare and her baby—those friends of my grandson. The man need not have died. I understand he loved his son."

Again Maria Elena raised her bony arm to wave away her daughter's objection. "That man brought on his own death. I did nothing but pave his way to hell."

Lupe did not wish to argue with her mother today. Maria Elena looked unwell. Lupe had come to turn her mother away from her own path to hell.

"Mama, I have good news to share. My son-in-law appears to be reforming his ways. He has performed a good deed. One that took real effort on his part."

Maria Elena stared out into the rainforest with one of her blank stares and Lupe knew her mother was seeing in her mind what Brody Ryan had done thousands of miles away.

"So… The man who cast you out has taken another's side, and at some personal expense. What is this to me?"

Sighing and wishing that her mother could find a little of the old kindness she remembered from long ago, Lupe chose her words carefully. "I wondered if his change of heart would change your heart, as well. Perhaps—"

"Nonsense. One good deed does not erase the black marks on the soul of that man."

Lupe wished with all her heart to find a way to erase the black marks on her mother's soul.

She cleared her throat and began again, "Perhaps not. But

would it not indicate that he may be worthy of redemption if he continues on his new course?"

"Why do you care about this man?"

"I do not. I care for my grandchildren who did no wrong and were made a part of his curse. I seek a way of redemption for them through him."

For the first time in more years than Lupe could remember, her mother's cold, hard stare softened—just a fraction.

"Your grandchildren have inherited the magic?"

"Yes, Mama."

"Then, very well. If their father can accomplish two more good deeds of the same magnitude, I will consider reversing the curse."

It was a better offer than nothing, and Lupe rejoiced at the opportunity. Now all Brody Ryan had to do was find enough of a heart to perform two more good deeds.

Lupe only wished she had more faith that he would.

Josh slammed Lucille into Park and raced up the flagstone path to his father's front door. Just as his fist slammed down on the ornately carved wood, the door opened. His father stood there, hat and keys in hand.

"Dad, are you going somewhere?" Josh wanted to ask for his father's help, but he needed his full attention.

"Uh…yeah," Brody told his son. "But your sister already called ahead. I know what you want and I can take a moment out for you. You can have whatever you need. Figure out how much money you want and let me know. It'll be yours after I die anyway."

"Oh." Josh had been prepared for an argument, and now he didn't know what to say. "Thanks." But that didn't seem enough somehow.

Maybe he should try to be a little friendlier if his father intended to be so amiable. "Um. Where're you headed?"

Brody looked down at the hat in his hand. "Aw. It's nothing

much. Just got word there's a couple of squatters over at the old homestead. I was headed over there to check it out."

When Brody looked up, Josh could swear there was a grin hiding behind the serious look on his father's face before the old man spoke again. "Look, you could do me a big favor and run this chore for me. I have a dozen other things on my plate for the afternoon."

"Oh? Well, sure. I guess. The house belongs to us kids now anyway. I suppose it's kind of my job."

Instead of a discussion about who owned the old Delgado homestead as he'd thought they might have, his father just nodded and said, "Thanks. Get on over there now. And be sure to let me know whatever you need. *When* you figure it out, that is."

Shaking his head, Josh turned around and headed back to his pickup. Well, that was sure weird. But he didn't intend to stop and dwell on it at the moment.

Somehow squatters had gotten through all the Delgado security. Probably drug runners. Josh stopped only long enough to check and load the shotgun he'd hung over Lucille's back window. When he was ready, he swung into the driver's seat and took off.

Those squatters were about to find out whose property they'd dared to cross.

When Clare heard a motor racing up the lane toward the house, her pulse picked up. She and Jimmy had been cleaning out the kitchen cabinets and she looked a wreck. Running a hand over her hair to smooth down the flyaway strands, she wondered who was heading their way.

Thinking about who it was she wanted to see the most, Clare grabbed Jimmy off the floor and walked toward the front door. She didn't know whether she wanted it to be him or not. So far she'd deliberately avoided any contact. But they'd only just arrived this morning and she guessed maybe her hesitation had been a case of lost nerves.

Her arguments were all in place. She'd rehearsed and practiced them until her voice was hoarse. Still, as she peeked out through the front windows, her legs wobbled and her hands shook.

Then, there he was. He pulled Lucille right up in front of the door and climbed out with a shotgun in his hands. *A shotgun?*

"You in there," he called out. Then he said the same thing again in Spanish.

It was a good thing Clare had taken the time to learn a little more Spanish while staying at his Abuela's home. He obviously didn't know she and Jimmy were inside and she needed to explain. But as he stood with his legs spread and steadied the shotgun in the crook of his arm, her mind blanked and her mouth went dry.

She'd missed the sound of his voice, the power and courage in it. His warm smiles. And the intensity she'd felt in his arms that had given her a solid strength, so much so it had seen her through the toughest hours. For all these weeks she had craved his smiles, his touch, his voice. And there he was, only a few feet away.

Trembling, not with fear but with need, she coughed and then called out, "It's us, Josh. Do you intend to shoot us?"

The gun lowered in his hands, but he still looked wary. "Come out."

Clare opened the door and carried Jimmy out onto the porch. "Hi."

Josh's mouth dropped open. He quickly fixed something on the gun and stowed it in Lucille's cab. Slamming the truck's door behind him, he moved in their direction, slowly at first and then at a run.

"Clare! Jimmy!" He drew them both into his embrace, lifting Clare off her feet, and spun them both around.

Setting her back on her feet, he gulped in a breath and then blinked his eyes as if he couldn't believe what he was seeing. "What are you doing here?"

"Your father said it would be all right if we stayed here…at least for a while. I know this place is more yours than his. I hope that's okay with you."

"My father?" Josh narrowed his eyes for a second. "That son of a bitch. I almost shot you."

"Josh, please be careful what you say around Jimmy. He's picking up everything he hears these days. You watch, he'll be saying that word later today." But Jimmy wasn't saying anything at the moment. He stared at Josh as if he'd seen a ghost.

With her heart in her throat, Clare tried to placate Josh. "If you don't want us here, we'll go. Just give me a few days to—"

"Not want you?" He was shaking his head as if he still couldn't understand what was happening. "What are you doing here in Texas instead of in Mexico?"

"Didn't anyone tell you?" At his blank look, she went on. "Your father has been just wonderful. He loaned Jimmy and I money when we started off to Mexico. And then yesterday he called to tell us we're in the clear. Apparently he's got a lot of contacts in Washington and he made some kind of arrangement about that oil treaty."

Josh still looked shocked, so she continued, "Actually I think he must have threatened to cut off some of his gas wells and slow down a couple of refineries if our government finalized the deal with Ramzi's father. I guess the Abu Fujarah government has been subsidizing terrorists and your father pointed that out, too. I don't know all the details. But the State Department says I'm free to naturalize Jimmy anytime I want now and our status in the U.S. is guaranteed.

"Ramzi's father is welcome to visit Jimmy, but we stay in America. I have the law on my side."

Josh fisted his hands and crammed them on his hips. "So it's all over. You're free. And my father managed it himself?"

He didn't look too happy, and it made Clare's stomach knot.

She'd had such wonderful dreams of them being together since there was no longer any danger. Now, she wasn't sure of anything.

She stepped close and laid her hand on his cheek. "You haven't kissed me yet. Does that mean you want us to go? I'd thought… I hoped…"

Looking frustrated and dismal, Josh turned his chin and softly placed a kiss into her open palm. "You and Jimmy can stay as long as you want. But you'd be a lot better off in a bigger city. One where there's available men for you to meet."

"Available *men?*" Anger rose hot and quick, flashing over all the tender feelings and lovely expectations. "Are you trying to get rid of me? Well darn it, you are just going to have to say it plain enough so I can understand.

"I came here hoping we could all move into this old place together," she continued, slowly and deliberately. "Make a family. Jimmy needs a dad. I need a husband and you…" Tears ran down her cheeks and her voice cracked with emotion.

Jimmy began to fuss and squirm in her arms. He was catching the mood of the two adults and matching it.

"Exactly," Josh broke in dejectedly. "You need a husband who can give you all the children you want. That's not me. There's a curse—"

She stepped back, swiped at her eyes and waved her hand to make him stop talking. "I know all about the story of the curse. And after meeting your grandmother, I've decided it must be true. But if you think for one minute that not being able to have more children matters to me even a little bit…"

Taking another step back from him, Clare had to fight the flood of tears threatening to choke her words and cause a complete breakdown. "Just how shallow do you think I am? That I would marry some man I didn't even love with all my heart just so he could father a bunch of kids?"

"But I thought having a lot of children was the most important thing to you." Josh lifted his hand toward her hesitantly, but quickly dropped it again. "I want you to be happy. I want your life to turn out like you dreamed."

That did it. Jimmy was whining full out now and the tears rolled down Clare's face like a rain shower. The man was being impossible. And she would *not* have it!

Moving in closer, close enough to see the sheen of tears in his eyes, Clare grabbed the front of his shirt. "I love you, you foolish man. With all my heart. We can adopt kids. Or we can just raise Jimmy and be proud parents of an only child. It doesn't matter, not as long as we're together."

Josh searched her eyes and she hoped he was looking for the truth. But he didn't say a word.

On a sob and with the most raspy voice in history, Clare gave it one last shot. "Joshua Ryan. Either tell me you love me, too, and come inside, or tell me goodbye."

As a tear leaked from the corner of his eye, Josh bent his head and placed the most gentle of all kisses against her lips. Clare wondered if it was his way of saying he loved her, or his way of saying goodbye. The tension in her body was strung tight enough to crack her in two.

Pulling his head back slightly, he studied her face. "I love you, Clare. You and Jimmy have become my life. If you're willing— stay. Stay with me in this house and let's make a family together. Whether it's three people or ten, our family will always be filled with love. Always. I swear I will love you and Jimmy for as long as I'm breathing."

She couldn't manage a word. Just pulled his head back down for another kiss. This time she put her heart and body behind it. Clare poured all the pent-up love she'd been saving into telling him without words how she felt.

After a dream-filled few minutes, Josh lifted his head, took a breath and looked at Jimmy. "Let's not forget you, partner. You're part of this family, too. How do you feel about me?" He held out his arms, coaxing Jimmy to come to him.

Jimmy reared back, looked at both his mother and Josh and finally lifted his arms to Josh. "Love you."

Josh took him and chuckled. "I love you, too, son."

Jimmy patted his cheek and squealed in delight. "Son a' bitch!"

Epilogue

On a sunny June fifteenth two people—one who'd been running from a dangerous ex-husband and one who'd been running from his life—married and, together with her son, became a family. Josh and Clare said their vows on the flagstone steps of his father's home as Josh held Jimmy in his arms. Then the whole wedding party moved over to the old Delgado homestead for a Texas barbecue.

Yellow-and-white wildflowers waved in the brisk breeze on the south Texas plain. Family, neighbors and friends celebrated with cold longnecks and roasted meat while the family's recently purchased horse stock gallivanted in the pasture nearby.

Josh carried Jimmy on his hip as he greeted everyone. He'd been pleasantly surprised to meet Clare's father at last, and they'd found they had more in common than just a love of Clare and Jimmy. But as Josh moved about the crowds of mostly his own relatives, he never lost track of Clare. He could scarcely believe his terrific luck. Just to think—a loner who for all his life had been ashamed of his heritage now had so many great reasons to stand proud.

Clare and Maggie strolled up to Josh and Maggie pulled Jimmy into her arms. "Hey, big boy. You going to become a Ryan now, too, like your mommy?"

Jimmy nodded and then pointed at the colts and fillies in the pasture. "Horsey!"

Everyone laughed as Clare quietly slid her arms around Josh's waist. The zing of awareness was always there between them, and he had to take a breath in order to keep talking like an intelligent being. The end of this party couldn't come too soon for him.

"Where's your baby, Mags?" he managed.

"Lara has Emma," Maggie told him as she bounced Jimmy and whispered in his ear. "Everyone's been passing her around. She's such a good baby."

Josh knew his sister wouldn't stop looking for little Emma's relatives. But he also knew she would rather not find them. In the meantime, her searches were helping to make their family's new bodyguarding business boom.

Maggie set Jimmy down on his feet and the boy took off running across the yard. "I'll keep an eye on him. But he really wants to play with the other kids. Okay?"

Clare nodded and smiled but also kept an eye on her son.

"I sure wish Grandpa and Nana Ryan were here. They always loved having lots of kids around." Maggie's words were mellow, melancholy. "And I'm sorry Abuela Lupe couldn't make it to the wedding. I'd love to see her again."

Josh nodded at his sister's words. "She has a full life in Mexico now. But I have a feeling she's been watching today. Don't you feel it, too?"

Maggie also nodded, just as she spied Jimmy racing toward

the pasture. "I'll get him. Don't worry." She took off at a run, yelling for Jimmy at the top of her lungs.

Laughing, Josh pulled Clare close and planted a big, wet kiss on her lips. "Hey, Mrs. Ryan. I was just thinking that you can keep your fake driver's license now. It's got the right name on it at last."

Clare grinned. "You are a wicked, wicked man, Josh Ryan. I'll be getting a legal license…when I'm ready."

He tilted his head and tried to keep a straight face, loving her reactions to being teased. "You already having second thoughts about becoming Clare Ryan?"

With her own teasing smile, Clare raised her eyebrows and threw his words back at him. "Yeah, that's likely."

She eased her hands down his chest and let her fingers glide under his belt. "When my hands stop wanting to touch you. Maybe. Or when my heart stops flipping every time you look at me. Maybe then. But not before."

"Hey," he said as her fingers burned a path lower and lower. "I'll give you exactly sixty years to quit that."

But there would be no quitting, he knew. Not with the kind of love that bound them together.

Their kind of love had magic. For now and for always.

* * * * *

*Josh and Clare found that the magic of love
can overcome all things. But what about the other Ryans?
Look for Ethan's story, SAFE BY HIS SIDE,
the next in Linda Conrad's wonderful miniseries*
THE SAFEKEEPERS,
*in October 2008.
Only from Silhouette Romantic Suspense!*

Dear Reader,

I've gone back to my Texas roots in writing this new series about a cursed family. Dysfunctional families are always fun to write, and this one was no exception. But the Ryan-Delgado family is exceptional. This Texas family can actually perform witchcraft! Isn't that an interesting idea? Who wouldn't love having the ability to put a curse on mean cousin Agatha, or creepy uncle Combover?

As I wrote THE SAFEKEEPERS trilogy, I also wanted to explore what it means to be a woman. I came up with three traits I thought were representative of the best of womankind: courage, motherhood and love. In this first book, Clare Chandler finds out just how far she will go in order to protect her child. She faces difficulty, danger and the pain of loss—gladly—in order to give her son the chance he needs to lead a life full of love. She is the embodiment of feminine courage and strength. She is Woman.

The next book in the trilogy, *Safe by His Side,* will continue my quest with the story of a woman who agrees to become the substitute mother of a child in danger. Blythe Cooper goes through a lot to find her path to motherhood, and she needs someone like Ethan Ryan to show the way.

I hope you've enjoyed reading Josh and Clare's story and meeting the Ryan-Delgado family. And I hope you'll look for the second book in the trilogy to see how the Delgado curse unfolds!

With all my best,

Linda

The editors at Harlequin Blaze have never been afraid to push the limits—tempting readers with the forbidden, whetting their appetites with a wide variety of story lines. But now we're breaking the final barrier—the time barrier.

In July, watch for BOUND TO PLEASE by fan favorite Hope Tarr, Harlequin Blaze's first ever historical romance—a story that's truly Blaze-worthy in every sense.

Here's a sneak peek…

BRIANNA stretched out beside Ewan, languid as a cat, and promptly fell asleep. Midday sunshine streamed into the chamber, bathing her lovely, long-limbed body in golden light, the sea-scented breeze wafting inside to dry the damp red-gold tendrils curling about her flushed face. Propping himself up on one elbow, Ewan slid his gaze over her. She looked beautiful and whole, satisfied and sated, and altogether happier than he had so far seen her. A slight smile curved her beautiful lips as though she must be in the midst of a lovely dream. She'd molded her lush, lovely body to his and laid her head in the curve of his shoulder and settled in to sleep beside him. For the longest while he lay there turned toward her, content to watch her sleep, at near perfect peace.

Not wholly perfect, for she had yet to answer his marriage

proposal. Still, she wanted to make a baby with him, and Ewan no longer viewed her plan as the travesty he once had. He wanted children—sons to carry on after him, though a bonny little daughter with flame-colored hair would be nice, too. But he also wanted more than to simply plant his seed and be on his way. He wanted to lie beside Brianna night upon night as she increased, rub soothing unguents into the swell of her belly, knead the ache from her back and make slow, gentle love to her. He wanted to hold his newly born child in his arms and look down into Brianna's tired but radiant face and blot the perspiration from her brow and be a husband to her in every way.

He gave her a gentle nudge. "Brie?"

"Hmm?"

She rolled onto her side and he captured her against his chest. One arm wrapped about her waist, he bent to her ear and asked, "Do you think we might have just made a baby?"

Her eyes remained closed, but he felt her tense against him. "I don't know. We'll have to wait and see."

He stroked his hand over the flat plane of her belly. "You're so small and tight it's hard to imagine you increasing."

"All women increase no matter how large or small they start out. I may not grow big as a croft, but I'll be big enough, though I have hopes I may not waddle like a duck, at least not too badly."

The reference to his fair-day teasing was not lost on him. He grinned. "Brianna MacLeod has grown so large she must sit still for once in her life. I'll need the proof of my own eyes to believe it."

Despite their banter, he felt his spirits dip. Assuming they were so blessed, he wouldn't have the chance to see her thus. By then he would be long gone, restored to his clan according to the sad bargain they'd struck. He opened his mouth to ask her to marry him again and then clamped it closed, not wanting to spoil the moment, but the unspoken words weighed like a millstone on his heart.

The damnable bargain they'd struck was proving to be a devil's pact indeed.

* * * * *

*Will these two star-crossed lovers find their
sexily-ever-after?
Find out in BOUND TO PLEASE by Hope Tarr,
available in July
wherever Harlequin® Blaze™ books are sold.*

Harlequin Blaze marks new territory with its first historical novel!

For years readers have trusted the Harlequin Blaze series to entertain them with a variety of stories— Now Blaze is breaking down the final barrier— the time barrier!

Welcome to Blaze Historicals—all the sexiness you love in a Blaze novel, all the adventure of a historical romance. It's the best of both worlds!

Don't miss the first book in this exciting new miniseries:

BOUND TO PLEASE
by Hope Tarr

New laird Brianna MacLeod knows she can't protect her land or her people without a man by her side. So what else can she do—she kidnaps one! Only, she doesn't expect to find herself the one enslaved....

Available in July wherever Harlequin books are sold.

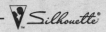

SPECIAL EDITION™

NEW YORK TIMES BESTSELLING AUTHOR

DIANA PALMER

A brand-new Long, Tall Texans novel

HEART OF STONE

Feeling unwanted and unloved, Keely returns
to Jacobsville and to Boone Sinclair, a rancher
troubled by his own past. Boone has always
seemed reserved, but now Keely discovers a
sensuality with him that quickly turns to love. Can
they each see past their own scars to let love in?

Available September 2008
wherever you buy books.

REQUEST YOUR FREE BOOKS!

2 FREE NOVELS PLUS 2 FREE GIFTS!

Silhouette® Romantic

SUSPENSE

Sparked by Danger, Fueled by Passion!

YES! Please send me 2 FREE Silhouette® Romantic Suspense novels and my 2 FREE gifts (gifts are worth about $10). After receiving them, if I don't wish to receive any more books, I can return the shipping statement marked "cancel." If I don't cancel, I will receive 4 brand-new novels every month and be billed just $4.24 per book in the U.S. or $4.99 per book in Canada, plus 25¢ shipping and handling per book plus applicable taxes, if any*. That's a savings of at least 15% off the cover price! I understand that accepting the 2 free books and gifts places me under no obligation to buy anything. I can always return a shipment and cancel at any time. Even if I never buy another book from Silhouette, the two free books and gifts are mine to keep forever.

240 SDN EEX6 340 SDN EEYJ

Name _____ (PLEASE PRINT) _____

Address _____ Apt. # _____

City _____ State/Prov. _____ Zip/Postal Code _____

Signature (if under 18, a parent or guardian must sign)

Mail to the **Silhouette Reader Service:**
IN U.S.A.: P.O. Box 1867, Buffalo, NY 14240-1867
IN CANADA: P.O. Box 609, Fort Erie, Ontario L2A 5X3

Not valid to current subscribers of Silhouette Romantic Suspense books.

Want to try two free books from another line?
Call 1-800-873-8635 or visit www.morefreebooks.com.

* Terms and prices subject to change without notice. N.Y. residents add applicable sales tax. Canadian residents will be charged applicable provincial taxes and GST. Offer not valid in Quebec. This offer is limited to one order per household. All orders subject to approval. Credit or debit balances in a customer's account(s) may be offset by any other outstanding balance owed by or to the customer. Please allow 4 to 6 weeks for delivery. Offer available while quantities last.

Your Privacy: Silhouette is committed to protecting your privacy. Our Privacy Policy is available online at www.eHarlequin.com or upon request from the Reader Service. From time to time we make our lists of customers available to reputable third parties who may have a product or service of interest to you. If you would prefer we not share your name and address, please check here. ☐

SRS08R

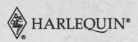

HARLEQUIN®

American ★ Romance®

DOUBLE THE REASONS
TO PARTY!

**We are celebrating American Romance's
25th Anniversary just in time to make
your Fourth of July celebrations
sensational with Kraft!**

American Romance is presenting
four fabulous recipes from Kraft,
to make sure your Fourth of July
celebrations are a hit! Each
American Romance book in June contains a different
recipe—a salad, appetizer, main course or a dessert.
Collect all four in June wherever books are sold!

kraftfoods.com—
deliciously simple. everyday.

Or visit kraftcanada.com
for more delicious meal ideas.

www.eHarlequin.com   KRAFTBPA

Silhouette®
Romantic
SUSPENSE

COMING NEXT MONTH

#1519 A SOLDIER'S HOMECOMING—Rachel Lee
Conard County: The Next Generation
When he learns the truth about his father, military man Ethan Parish
is determined to reunite with his long-lost family in Wyoming. On his
way into town, he clashes with policewoman Connie Halloran, whose
captivating beauty entices him. Together, they confront the dangers
inherent in family secrets.

#1520 KILLER PASSION—Sheri WhiteFeather
Seduction Summer
Racked with guilt over his wife's murder, Agent Griffin Malone tries to get
his life back on track. Enter Alicia Greco, an attractive and accomplished
analyst for a travel company. The two meet and find passion, which is
exactly what puts them into a serial killer's sights. Will they escape the
island's curse on lovers?

#1521 SNOWBOUND WITH THE BODYGUARD—Carla Cassidy
Wild West Bodyguards
Single mom Janette Black needs to protect her baby from repeated
threats by the girl's father. Fleeing for their lives, she knows bodyguard
Dalton West is the only man who can help. After taking them in, they brave
a snowstorm and discover a sense of home. This time, can Janette trust that
she's found the perfect sanctuary...and lasting love?

#1522 DUTY TO PROTECT—Beth Cornelison
Crisis counselor Ginny West is trapped in an office fire when firefighter
Riley Sinclair walks into her life. A bond forms between the two,
especially when he keeps saving her from a menacing client. As danger
still looms, one defining moment forces the pair to reassess their
combustible relationship.

SRSCNM0608